Evergreen Dreams

Rachel M. Hay

Rachel M. Hay
Xenia, OH

ISBN 978-0-615-71081-5

Library of Congress Control Number: 2012919329

All scripture quotations are taken from the King James Version of the Bible.

This book is a work of fiction. Names, characters, places, and incidents are either products of the author's imagination or used fictitiously. Any similarity to actual people, organizations, and/or events is purely coincidental.

Published by Rachel M. Hay

First printing: December 2012 (100 copies)

Printed in the United States of America

Printing by Morris Publishing®
3212 E. Highway 30
Kearney, NE 68847
1-800-650-7888
www.morrispublishing.com

Author photo by: betterImages portrait studio

Publisher's Cataloging-in-Publication
(Provided by Quality Books, Inc.)

Hay, Rachel M.
Evergreen dreams / Rachel M. Hay.
p. cm.
LCCN 2012919329
ISBN 978-0-615-71081-5

1. Newlyweds--Fiction. 2. Soldiers--Fiction.
3. Families--Fiction. 4. Love stories, American.
5. Christian fiction, American. I. Title.

PS3608.A899E95 2012 813'.6
QBI12-600210

Acknowledgments

I would like to thank my husband, Nathan, who has consistently encouraged me to pursue my dream of writing. Your support has made all the difference!

I would also like to thank my mom, who has encouraged my storytelling since I was five years old.

The Lord is my light and my salvation;
whom shall I fear?
the Lord is the strength of my life;
of whom shall I be afraid?
Psalm 27:1

For thou art my hope, O Lord God:
thou art my trust from my youth.
Psalm 71:5

One

A New Beginning

"Here we go!" Graham Randall called back to the passengers riding behind him. After navigating his cherry sports car onto a rugged street, Graham laid down hard on the accelerator.

"Graham, not so fast!" Jared protested, raising his voice to cover the noise of the engine. "You'll make my new bride sick."

"I was just giving you a little foretaste of marriage," Graham answered, after starting to brake a few seconds too late before the next stop light. "You thought life moved quickly before...just wait!" A wide smile spread across Graham's tanned dark face, but he could tell by a glance in the rear view mirror that he was the only one enjoying himself.

"Please, Graham," Molly spoke up meekly, her hazel eyes soft and pleading, "my stomach is already a wreck."

"And we don't want to end up in one on our wedding day," Jared quickly added, putting his arm around Molly's shoulder.

"All right," Graham muttered, almost inaudibly to the couple behind him. Increasing his volume, he added, "I'll drive responsibly from here on and leave you two lovebirds alone."

Turning to Molly, Jared whispered, "I'm sorry. Maybe having my cousin drive us wasn't the best idea." His breath felt warm on Molly's neck and sent a tingle up her spine. Although she had been a little angered by Graham's "lesson", any lingering sparks were quickly extinguished by Jared's cool smile and soft touch on her shoulder.

"That's okay," she answered calmly. "He was just having fun and, besides, he did have the coolest car." Molly inhaled deeply, then let out a sigh. For the first moment that day she could truly be at ease.

"How do you feel?" Jared asked, gently fingering one of Molly's soft curls.

"Relieved," was Molly's honest reply.

"Why do you say that?" Jared coughed. "Did you think I was going to be a runaway groom or something?" Jared's turquoise-blue eyes danced as he spoke. No longer wearing his Air Force uniform, he too felt more carefree.

"Of course not," Molly answered quickly, before becoming more serious. "It's just that there are so many details to a wedding, so many chances for something to go wrong. I'm glad everything worked out pretty well. Krissie could have thrown her flower petals a little faster, but other than that..."

"I think she thought she was the one getting married instead of her big sister."

"Well, Krissie's always loved the spotlight." Molly leaned her head against Jared's shoulder, thankful for the quiet, smooth car ride they were now enjoying.

"You know what, honey?" Jared asked, again in a whisper.

"What?" Molly answered as softly as she could. She was expecting Jared to say something about their new status as husband and wife, so his answer caught her completely off guard.

"I think you worry too much." After kissing his bride's head, Jared began stroking her mass of curls. Molly relished the attention, but Jared's words continued to ring in her ears.

He's right, she told herself. *How will I ever manage when he goes if I was that worried about wedding details?*

Becoming distracted by the scenery around her, Molly wondered what it would be like to live in a place where nothing looked familiar. After spending her entire twenty-one years in the same, small Missouri town, she seemed to know every street and landmark within thirty miles of home. So many buildings were full of memories for her: the fifties' diner where her family used to celebrate special occasions, the library where she shelved books as a teenager, the park where Jared popped the question. *In time, Illinois will feel like home*, Molly reassured herself.

"I with I could get married," Krissie Evergreen sighed, trying to sound as mature as her seven years and recurring lisp would allow. As she spoke, Krissie shook the blond curls that framed her round face. Her hair, though somewhat flattened from a good night's sleep, was still arranged in ringlets as it had been the previous day when she had acted out the part of flower girl in her elder sister's wedding. *Acted* was right. Krissie's family had never seen her so excited.

Helen Evergreen, on the other hand, found herself on the opposite side of the emotional spectrum. Although she had loved Jared as a son for some time and knew that he would claim her daughter's hand *someday*, she struggled to accept how quickly that *someday* had come. The five short months spent preparing for Molly's wedding had seemed like a fleeting haze. Helen asked herself where the time had gone and if it wouldn't be long before she found herself remembering Krissie's comment after she too had been given away.

Allowing her imagination to get the better of her, Helen looked to her husband and lamented, "There we go, Tim. I told you when we lost one we would lose them all."

Timothy Evergreen did not immediately respond to his wife. Instead, running his long, slender fingers through his blond-gray hair, he looked across the table to his youngest daughter. Krissie was perplexed by the silence surrounding her, but it did not trouble her enough to prevent her from enjoying Helen's delicious cinnamon apples while they were still warm.

The picture of her was so far from Helen's disturbing vision that Timothy had to restrain his laughter. He opened his mouth to offer some words of comfort, but was stopped short by a familiar tune echoing down the street outside.

"Ithe cream man, ithe cream man!" Krissie shouted excitedly, her lisp clearly present, despite the speech therapy she had undergone. "Can I get something, Mommy? Pleathe?"

Helen quickly handed some one-dollar bills to Krissie and her older brother, Alex, who were gone in a flash to make their favorite purchases. Helen knew better than to offer her other two children any money, since they had long since lost Krissie's enthusiasm for the ice cream man.

As always, Helen insisted that Alex and Krissie finish their dinners before eating their treats. When her two smiling children came inside, Helen put their desserts in the freezer and returned to her place at the table. She had completely forgotten her former empty-nest anxiety. Her husband, however, had not.

"You know you're right, honey," Timothy commented to his wife, reading the surprise and confusion in her eyes as he spoke. "One of these days, Krissie might just elope with the ice cream man."

Instantly, the memory of her previous comment came streaming back into Helen's mind. Recognizing her own foolishness, she now allowed herself to laugh easily. Helen's other children smiled, but Krissie appeared serious and reflective. Unable to understand the meaning of her father's words, and knowing that she was somehow involved in the joke, Krissie asked timidly what "elope" meant.

Helen hesitated to reply, and when at last she did she used a sentence that was all too familiar to Krissie's ears, "I'll explain it to you when you're older."

Krissie heaved a heavy sigh. "I'll have a lot to learn then," she thought to herself.

Two

Dreams to Dream

"Each day I see them they seem more beautiful than the day before," Molly whispered dreamily to her husband. Standing by Jared's side with her hand clasped in his, Molly watched as the rushing waters of the falls cascaded down to the valley below. For a moment, Molly could have almost deceived herself into believing that she and her husband were alone in a wonderful world all their own. Yet, the constant streams of motion she sensed around her, and the delighted voices of children and adults alike, brought her back to reality. The same scenic beauty that had persuaded Jared and Molly to choose the region as a honeymoon destination had attracted all sorts of other individuals as well. As Molly's eyes scanned her surroundings, she recognized the diversity of activities in which the other tourists were engaged. Some were actively taking pictures, seeking to preserve what they could of the panorama before them. Others, in contrast, seemed to be merely using the falls as a backdrop for their conversations. Mothers and fathers with small children in their arms or on their shoulders were pointing out the falls to their wide-eyed youngsters. Couples both young and old were standing hand in hand, admiring the beauty displayed before them. A number of people were remarking about the heat. Many walked away sooner than they had anticipated in search of some shelter and shade. The day was certainly mild, as only a handful of clouds were present to obstruct the rays of the warm summer sun, but the cool mist brushing past Molly's face left her feeling relatively comfortable.

When Jared did not respond immediately to her comment, Molly continued, "Is that even possible? Can they become more beautiful every day, or am I just being silly?" There was only a slight degree of seriousness in her tone.

Now that Molly had specifically asked for his opinion, Jared quickly formulated a response. "I don't see why they couldn't become more beautiful," he said smiling.

Instinctively shifting her gaze from the falls to Jared, Molly waited for him to continue. She had little idea what he would say next. His eyes, like hers, were shielded behind sunglasses that kept expression at a minimum. Molly was both surprised and embarrassed when Jared spoke up to finish his thought.

Although his previous words had been uttered in his usual tone of voice, he now spoke in a hushed tone that signified his words were meant for only one listener, "After all, I know that you do."

Jared's words gave Molly the sort of tingling sensation she had experienced during their courtship when Jared had said similar things to her. She was glad that feeling still came now that they were married. Molly knew that she was blushing, but any bystander might have attributed the color on her cheeks to the warmth of the day. Still, Jared recognized that he had sufficiently unsettled Molly's mind by his compliment when she labored in silence to find something to say. He was pleased he continued to possess a power to set her speechless.

Unable to do anything but change the subject, Molly commented, "It hardly seems possible that we've been here five days already." Her words were hinged with a bit of sadness, as she remembered that the following day she and Jared would be returning to Illinois. Amazed at the passage of time, Molly turned her head and once more focused her gaze on the falls. By thwarting an answer to Jared's compliment, she had mistakenly chosen a dismal topic on which to meditate.

Jared was also sorry to recognize that their brief honeymoon was coming to an end. Their time together had been special for more than one reason. For much of the last year, Jared and Molly had been separated. Since graduating from basic training the previous autumn, Jared had been working in Illinois, while Molly had remained in her home state of Missouri. During most of their time apart, Jared and Molly kept in touch via e-mail and phone. They had seen each other only on a handful of weekends, when one of them was able to make the five-hour journey for love's sake. Since getting engaged over Christmas, Jared and Molly had not seen each other for more than two days at a time, and had been forced to make most wedding arrangements long-distance.

While their relationship before marriage had existed under the stress and strain of much time apart, their relationship as man and wife would, for a definite length of time, be marked by complete separation. Although their meetings in the past had been infrequent, they would be nonexistent as long as Jared was stationed in Iraq. Neither Jared nor Molly spoke much on the subject during their honeymoon, since both were afraid to poison time that was so precious. Instead, they had been allowing themselves to be caught up in the present. Yet, as Molly had mentioned, time was steadily moving forward. This very day they would have to start packing for their trip home tomorrow. Jared could not keep his heart from sinking under the weight of his reflections. It was apparent that sooner, rather than later, he and Molly would have to begin preparing themselves for a much lonelier reality than the one they were currently enjoying.

When Molly did not speak again for an extended length of time, Jared asked, "Are you happy...Mrs. Weaver?" He had begun his inquiry in all sincerity, but threw in the last two words to lighten the conversation.

Molly could not help but be pleased by Jared's address. Although she knew Jared had not used her new title seriously, she was still proud to hear it mentioned. She answered him honestly, expanding upon the formal dialog he had initiated.

"Yes, sir. Very happy indeed," she replied smiling. Her heart was once again light. At that moment all danger and heartache, whether real and imagined, seemed miles away. Everything around her appeared vibrant and full of life, from the excited children running back and forth, to the rushing falls that were from moment to moment changing in appearance, yet from day to day remaining the same. As Jared reached out his arm to pull Molly close to his chest, he found himself savoring a sort of silence which could not be made more meaningful by any number of words.

As she bent over to load some towels in the dryer, Helen Evergreen let out a little sigh. Although she sought to keep her mind and body occupied in order to keep her thoughts from centering on her recent adjustment, it seemed like every task brought back memories of Molly. Already Helen had found that baking reminded her of Molly's childhood cooking experiments, and the indigestion she and Timothy had suffered after sampling her creations. To Helen, it seemed a persistent and cruel reminder of Molly's absence whenever the table was set for six instead of seven. Now, Helen discovered that she could not even find sanctuary while managing the laundry. Memories of her lately married daughter seemed to surface everywhere, and although Helen was convinced that Jared and Molly were truly meant for each other, her happiness concerning Molly's marriage could not be wholly untouched by personal regret.

Unable to drive away memories that seemed to shadow her every move, Helen gave in and allowed herself to recall past events. Although nineteen years had since passed, Helen vividly remembered taking Molly with her to the laundry room in their former apartment building. At the time, Molly was Helen's only child. Molly always asked if she could help her mother with her task, and it became tradition that Helen would hand Molly the wet laundry to put into the dryer. Molly was, as Helen remembered her, not even the height of the dryer. Yet, her eyes would sparkle as she smiled at her mother, delighted she had been allowed to help. Helen could still picture her little figure crouching beside the appliance, and hear her high-pitched voice exclaiming in words that matched her size how cold the wet laundry that she handled was.

"You're being ridiculous," Helen told herself, as she rubbed the back of her hand across cheeks that had become damp with tears. "You've known this time would come," she continued in reproof, although it did little to lift her spirits.

Although Molly was no longer home to require Helen's care and attention, Helen still found herself busy tending to her four other children and her husband. She was glad that they yet depended upon her. While Maddy and Kevin were largely adults by merits of character and behavior, if not age, Alex and Krissie still required their mother to do many things for them. Helen had been a housewife ever since the time of Molly's birth. More than two decades later, she was a veteran in nearly everything pertaining to family and home.

While she was so absorbed in her reflections, Helen failed to recognize the footsteps of someone approaching her from behind. Just as she was shutting the dryer door, she felt something squeeze her shoulder. Hastily standing erect while letting out a piercing scream, Helen managed to jar her neck. Although it started throbbing almost immediately, she had no mind to turn to it, still believing herself in harm's way. When she came to her senses, however, and recognized that her alleged assailant was none other than her husband, she reproached him severely.

"Don't ever sneak up on me like that again!" she dictated, in between deep breaths that revealed how shaken up she had been. Finding herself in no danger now, Helen turned her attention to her neck, or rather it drew her attention to itself. Helen quickly found that moving her neck to the right was out of the question; shooting pain stood as a sentry to block any such movement. Although she felt slightly embarrassed doing so, Helen repositioned her entire frame in order to look Timothy more clearly in the face.

Although he had come home in a good mood, owing to the surprise he had intended to give his wife, Timothy now half-regretted his enthusiasm. Rarely before had his expectations of an anticipated event, and its fulfillment in reality, opposed each other so decidedly. His pride had been injured, and his nerves were still recovering, as the sound of Helen's screaming continued to ring in his ears. He had had no intention of startling his wife, and Helen's implication of this having been his object only frustrated him further.

"I wasn't trying to sneak up on you," he quickly asserted in his own defense. "I thought for sure you'd have heard me open the door and Scout barking before I came in."

As Helen studied Timothy's expression, she recognized veiled hurt and confusion. Feeling she had interrupted him in some way by her reaction, Helen let her guard down and apologized.

"I'm sorry," she began in a subdued tone, while continuing to massage her aching neck. "I guess I just didn't expect you home so early."

"Well," Timothy uttered, as more of an acceptance of his wife's honest answer than as the beginning of a new thought. He waited a few moments before responding further. "I had a good reason for coming home early," he continued at last, now feeling easy enough to smile. He knew that when Helen was aware of his plan, she would find herself smiling too. He did not want to reveal it yet, however.

"Where are the kids?" he asked, leaving Helen to wonder what he had meant by his previous statement. She might have feared something unpleasant had occurred, but Timothy appeared too relaxed for that to be possible. Still, Helen's curious heart was not satisfied, and as she paused to analyze the situation, she delayed in answering her husband's inquiry.

"Oh," she exclaimed, after Timothy had been obliged to ask her again, "Maddy dropped Kevin off at the soccer fields, while she went to the mall with Wesley and some others. Alex and Krissie were invited to have dinner over at the Lakes' home.

I've been here all alone for the last half-an-hour." Helen did not mean her last sentence as a further reproach on Timothy, but he was half inclined to interpret it as such.

"Until someone came up behind you without any warning and scared you half-to-death," he added, as if continuing her narrative. Timothy found himself more able to sympathize with his wife's situation now that he had more of the facts. He vaguely remembered being told that all of their children would be gone for the evening, but he had not really considered any of the implications. With four children in the house, Helen would not normally have been startled by someone approaching her without warning. Yet, having considered her children gone and her husband still at work, Helen had reacted naturally to the situation.

"What did you mean when you said you had a good reason for coming home early?" Helen asked, unable to let the comment pass by without another thought. She did not care to dwell on her recent upset, although she knew that her neck would soon require some serious attention. Timothy could tell by the twinkle in his wife's eyes that she suspected he was up to something. She was a discerning woman; he could not give her any sort of a hint or else she might unravel the mystery while he still desired to keep it a secret. As if to signal an end to any more of her prodding questions, Timothy quickly held out the palm of his right hand. He assured her that he would tell her what he meant, but only after all their children had arrived home. Meanwhile he urged her to lie down and put something on her neck. Helen didn't resist his suggestion or his offer to heat up some leftovers for the both of them. Yet, even while her body rested, Helen's mind couldn't help pondering what Timothy might have up his sleeve.

It was hours later before Helen's curiosity was finally appeased. While she prided herself in enjoying surprises, Helen only liked those of which she was aware.

Alex and Krissie were the first to arrive home since they had an earlier curfew than their elder brother and sister. After being dropped off by the family who had invited them over, they immediately began telling their parents about their rare and exciting night out. Although Helen hoped she and Timothy had trained their children to behave well in others' homes, she always liked to ask them various questions about how they acted away from home. Having two witnesses to inquire of meant that the answers she received were more likely to be accurate. Yet, Helen sometimes thought she didn't need to worry about honesty wherever Krissie was concerned. The little girl didn't try to cover up the truth or her feelings when she was asked whether or not she and her brother had helped with the dishes.

"They wouldn't let us," she replied with satisfaction. When Krissie realized that her mother was not amused, her smile quickly slid off her face.

When Maddy and Kevin arrived home, they were surprised to hear that the rest of their family had been anxiously waiting for them to return. Yet, even after they had been home for nearly ten minutes, Timothy had come no closer to making his announcement than he had been when utilizing the excuse of desiring his family first assembled together. He did so mischievously wishing to cause Helen's curiosity to reach its limit. She would only stand for a minimal delay, however, and soon began reminding him that he now had no excuse to keep his news to himself.

"Well," he began, "the reason I wanted everyone here is because you're all involved in what I'm about to say in some way or another. Your mother..." Timothy paused to glance across at his wife and savor the last moment of his superior knowledge, "your mother and I are leaving on a trip tomorrow afternoon, and you will be here by yourselves for the weekend."

As the kids anticipated what it would be like having the house to themselves, Helen's mind sought to unravel the mysteries that were still left undone by Timothy's announcement. How had he managed to plan this so quickly? When had he made the reservations? What had possessed him to plan this weekend in the first place?

That night when Timothy and Helen were in the privacy of their own room, the remainder of the story was revealed. To Helen's surprise, Timothy had apparently made plans for their trip over a month in advance, even while Helen was in the midst of helping Molly prepare for her wedding.

"But why?" Helen inquired. Although she felt she probably knew the answer to her question, she wanted to be assured of it. After all, it would only give her opportunity to praise her husband. Sometimes she felt she could sincerely underestimate him.

Although Timothy had enjoyed surprising the entire family with his news, the part of his role that he had most anticipated acting out was this private conversation with his wife. He was pleased that after nearly twenty-five years of marriage he could still keep some of his secrets until he wished to make them known. It was worth it to go out of his way for the woman he loved, who he knew would appreciate all the effort it took for him to plan something memorable and then keep the knowledge concerning his plans to himself for any length of time. There had been many occasions in which Timothy had wished he could share his news; keeping agreeable secrets was always work for him. He had almost considered telling one of his older children, but felt that would only burden one of them also. Besides, he had known that Helen would find the news easier to accept if she found he had been keeping it to himself.

Timothy smiled across the room at his wife, who had begun putting her jewelry away after he hesitated in answering her simple question. When Helen realized that her husband's silence was to be taken as part of his response, she turned to look him in the face. The love and devotion she saw there left her feeling so blessed and undeserving of the attention she had unknowingly received.

"I knew how stressed out you were with all the wedding planning," Timothy began to explain. As he spoke, he began to walk toward Helen, who stood ready to welcome his approach. Putting his arms around her waist and gazing thoughtfully into her eyes, Timothy continued, "I wished there was something I could do to help, but I figured out that the time was just going to be stressful no matter what I did or didn't do. So I decided that after the stress was over, we should take a trip and relax. Almost as soon as the idea came into my head I made the plans. I hope you don't mind." Timothy uttered his last words sarcastically, but the twinkle in his eyes gave his true feelings away.

"Mind?" Helen asked rhetorically. "I don't mind one bit." Although she considered it insufficient thanks, Helen reached up to kiss her husband, who received her affection along with her glowing appreciation for his errand as the greatest tokens of gratitude a man could hope to receive.

Three

Scouting for Scout

Although Helen had some reservations about leaving her children for the weekend, she anticipated the time away with her husband too fully to allow herself many feelings of guilt. She and Timothy had left the kids before when Molly was still with them. Although Maddy was a few years younger, she was nonetheless capable of looking after her younger siblings, who, for the most part, respected her authority.

Madeline, or Maddy as she was universally called, had been in many ways a puzzle to her mother growing up. Although Molly had enjoyed playing inside with dolls, tea sets, and stuffed toys, Maddy was drawn to the outdoors. Molly had loved it when her mother dressed her up for church on Sundays, but Maddy had endured her mother's wardrobe selections only when necessary. Given the liberty to choose her own outfits, she nearly always decided on slacks and shirts over dresses.

While Molly's circles of friends would almost always be composed exclusively of girls, Maddy had preferred to pal around with the boys. It seemed more natural in some ways, as she shared more of their interests than she did with others of her own gender. She followed a number of sports, and would join in with the boys at recess and after school whenever she was allowed. Although Molly preferred to stay neat and clean, Maddy never let mud or dirt keep her from enjoying herself. While Helen could by no means favor one of her children over another, she definitely preferred doing Molly's laundry to that of her sister's. Maddy was interested in science and in nature, and was not one to let a dare pass her by unchallenged.

Even Maddy's features were characteristic of her personality. Her light auburn hair was given naturally to waves that, if not attended to properly, would easily become tangled and matted together. Since Maddy had a fondness for physical exertion, she most often kept her hair pulled up in some sort of knot behind her head. Maddy had taken her height from her father and, at five foot, eight inches tall, she easily overshadowed her more petite mother and elder sister. Her green eyes stood beneath almost transparently ruddy eyebrows on her oval face, which was narrow in the same way that the rest of her body was lean. Maddy had a pale complexion, but more often than not her face could be found decorated with freckles that told of her time spent in the sun.

Despite all their differences, Molly and Maddy had been as close of friends growing up as the disparities in their ages and interests would allow. Since the girls did not share the same goals or hobbies, it had been more difficult to compare their achievements, and they had experienced fewer feelings of rivalry toward one another than might have been the case had they been more alike.

Since Molly shared more of her mother's interests, she developed a closer bond with Helen than Maddy did. While Maddy was not deceptive, she did not choose to reveal as much to her mother as her sister was in the habit of doing. Either she kept her thoughts to herself, or she shared them with others. Whatever the case, Maddy did not seem to need the encouragement and support that Molly had required. Maddy exuded confidence, even in situations in which it was not particularly appropriate. When Helen left instructions for Maddy pertaining to different things that needed to be taken care of during her trip, she felt as if she were leaving them with an experienced adult, rather than with a seventeen-year-old who had never before been left solely in charge.

"Don't worry about anything," Maddy urged her mother as Helen said goodbye to each of her children. "I'll keep an eye on everything...and everyone." Maddy added her last words with a knowing glance at her younger brother, Alex, whom she figured was the most likely to concoct some form of mischief during her parents' absence. If Maddy had meant to restrain any of her brother's wild experiments by her gaze, her plan succeeded, as Alex never thought of doing anything out of the ordinary when he knew himself to be under close supervision. Yet, while Maddy anticipated a relaxed and carefree weekend in which no situation would arise to unsettle her, she found herself feeling on the very next day that her confidence in herself had been unmerited.

It was a typical Saturday just before the advent of summer. Only a few bands of clouds had courage enough to oppose the Sun's intense rays. Kevin and Alex were taking full advantage of the bright, clear day by playing football with some other boys down the street. Meanwhile, Krissie and Maddy were sitting indoors, the former playing with dolls, while the latter was flipping through some of her mother's magazines. Gazing across the room at the clock on the bookshelf, and finding the time to be almost five, however, Maddy quickly arose to make dinner for her siblings and herself. Although Helen had not expected Maddy to learn any new recipes during her absence, and offered several times to prepare meals in advance, Maddy was determined to try her hand at cooking. She always found it more enjoyable to perform a task when it was unexpected than when it was required. Unlike her older sister, Maddy had not had much experience in the kitchen, but she knew her mother might soon require her help on a regular basis, since Molly was no longer home to fulfill that role. In spite of herself, Maddy wished to feel as if she knew what she was doing in the kitchen even before being taught. She had borrowed one of her mother's cookbooks and determined to make homemade pizza. When she had informed her siblings of her plan, however, Maddy found that they did not possess the same degree of faith in her abilities as she did.

"You're going to cook?" Krissie had asked incredulously, her eyebrows raised in amusement. Considering how this substitution would affect the family's normal meal-time routine, Krissie continued, "Then who'th going to help me set the table?" Maddy had shared this task with her younger sister until the present time, yet, finding herself called to bigger and better things, she informed Krissie that she was old enough to handle the responsibility herself.

"What's on the menu?" Kevin inquired, curious to see how great a transformation in his sister he was about to witness. Good-humored by nature, Kevin was easily amused, but rarely sarcastic. His dark brown hair was naturally given to waves, which made each morning a struggle for him as he tried to iron them out. Kevin was still growing into his five-foot ten frame, but at a rapid pace. He had been enrolled in karate since he was Alex's age and now enjoyed teaching his beginner brother the basics he had learned a number of years ago. Although he was a few years younger than Maddy, the two were generally close, sharing many of the same interests.

"Homemade pizza," Maddy answered, with as much satisfaction as if she had already cooked the dish and placed it on the table for the others to taste and enjoy. Alex commented to the others that pizza was a good choice, and Maddy would have been pleased with his remark had she not managed to catch the explanation he gave after he thought his sister was out of hearing.

"Since we'll all be hungry for pizza, we can order one if Maddy's doesn't come out," he told his brother and sister, who tried not to laugh when Maddy turned around to glare at them.

In spite of the jokes she inspired, Maddy's cooking attempt proved to be a success. Although the sink was a mess, with dirty dishes and plates stacked up beyond the height of its faucet, the pizza crust was a beautiful golden-brown and the meal smelled as good as it looked. Maddy breathed a sigh of relief as she pulled it out of the oven. While she had enough confidence in herself to behave as if she knew what she were doing in the sight of others, she had secretly doubted her strengths and wondered, like Alex, if she would not be forced to call for back up at the end of it. Once she had proven herself, however, she began to regain her former confidence. She told Krissie that she was going down the street to find Alex and Kevin and tell them to come back home for dinner. Once outside, however, Maddy found that her brothers had already returned home. She caught a glimpse of them out of the corner of her eye as she started down the street. They were standing listlessly by the side of the house and seemed to have no other objective than occupying the space in which they stood. They were not talking or laughing or even moving. As she came nearer to them, Maddy traced the lines of fear and worry in their faces. Although Maddy's pulse began to quicken at the sight of them, she reasoned to herself that if anything serious had happened they would have sought her out immediately.

"What are you doing over here?" she asked, a tinge of anger apparent in her tone. When they did not respond, Maddy continued, "I was just coming out to look for you to tell you that dinner is done." When neither of her brothers responded, Maddy again became concerned. She had little idea what the problem might be, as every visible indicator testified to normalcy. Kevin and Alex looked the way they always did when they came back from playing football. Their pant legs were coated with dirt and mud and their shirts continued to cling to their chests. Their faces appeared red and smudged in places where they had apparently wiped their dirty hands across their eyes in order to see more clearly. Neither Kevin nor Alex seemed to be in any physical pain. The only thing that appeared at all out of place was that the side gate was standing open. Maddy spoke before considering what her questions might mean.

"Why's the gate open?" she asked. "Where's Scout?"

At this point Krissie had come out to join her sister in the side yard. When she saw the scene before her and caught the end of her older sister's words, Krissie began crying. Maddy looked to Kevin for an explanation.

"The gate didn't get latched all the way, I guess," he responded gravely. "Scout must have run away."

Maddy placed her hand against her forehead, where beads of sweat had begun to form. Her heart began beating faster, and she felt for a moment as if time were rapidly slowing down. *Scout ran away? This was so much worse than burning dinner! Where had her mind been? Why hadn't she been more careful?* As Maddy pondered all these things silently without thought to her immediate surroundings, she was startled by her younger sister, who ran to her side and hugged her.

"What are we going to do?" Krissie pleaded, looking up into her big sister's eyes. Maddy knew that she needed to be strong for Krissie's sake, although she loved Scout just as much as the others. He had been a Christmas present to all the kids three years ago. Since his arrival, Scout had filled the Evergreen household with a great deal of energy and joy. As a miniature schnauzer, he was generally kept inside. He only liked being outside for short periods of time. Knowing this, Maddy asked who had let him out last and when.

"I don't know," Kevin responded. Maddy began thinking back, hoping she would remember something that could be of use. She felt a pit form in her stomach when she remembered that she had let Scout outside about half-an-hour earlier. She had forgotten to check on him because she had been so absorbed in fixing dinner. Maddy reproached herself a hundred times while admitting to the others that she was to blame. Then they all began a form of action for rescuing their beloved companion.

It was decided that Kevin, Alex, and Krissie would go looking for Scout, while Maddy would remain at home to receive any calls they might receive about him. After half-an-hour of searching, the three members of the search party came home looking more wary and dispirited than before.

"Did you find him?" Maddy asked as they walked in the door. Originally her worst fear had been that they would be unable to find Scout. Recognizing the looks on their faces, however, Maddy was forced to consider an even more dreadful scenario. She was actually thankful when Kevin spoke up to inform her that they had found no trace of Scout. No news was perhaps good news indeed.

"We looked everywhere," Alex lamented, before heading to his room to avoid having his older brother witness him in tears.

"We knocked on everyone's door on these two blocks," Kevin told Maddy. "No one has seen him." Kevin could not blame Alex for escaping to their room. In some ways he wished he could join him. He had done what he could; now all he could do was wait and pray that Scout would be found soon and that he would be all right.

"It's all my fault," Maddy whispered despairingly. "Mom never would have forgotten she had let Scout outside. Maybe if we had started searching sooner we would have found him by now."

Neither Kevin nor Krissie responded immediately to their sister's remark. They did not blame Maddy for what had happened; they just wished they could do something to help. Finally, Krissie's voice broke through the drab silence in which the room had been engulfed.

"I know what we can do!" Krissie said enthusiastically. "We can put Scout's favorite treats out in the front yard. When he smells them, he's sure to come home!" Maddy wondered to herself whether or not such a plan was at all feasible since Scout might be any distance away from their house by now. Still, Krissie's idea involved action, and that was something Maddy's heart craved.

Krissie immediately went to work scattering dog biscuits across the front yard. Meanwhile, Maddy diced up some strawberries and put them on a plate alongside some small carrots. The front yard would mean a feast for Scout if he decided to return home.

"What are you doing?" Alex asked his brother and sisters after hearing the sound of their commotion from his room and following them outside to investigate. Krissie answered him with an air of superiority, taking advantage of the rare opportunity to be condescending to her older brother.

"*We're* trying to bring Scout back," she informed him.

"By scattering food in the front yard?" Alex questioned, appearing cynical just to irritate his little sister.

"Yes," Krissie replied, before entering a real debate with Alex. The two quarreled until Maddy finally thought to put an end to their dispute. Not only had she not looked after Scout, now she was failing to keep peace among her younger brother and sister. Maddy wasn't sure if she would ever be able to regain her confidence after this disastrous weekend.

When Kevin suggested that he should again go looking for Scout, Alex quickly volunteered to go with him. Krissie was just as pleased to stay home with Maddy and watch out the window until Scout should find his treats.

Another hour passed by without anyone hearing or seeing anything of Scout. Even Krissie began to fear that her plan was not as ingenious as she had previously thought. She was sitting on her knees against the back of the couch with her hands resting along its cushioned top. When she had first positioned herself at this outpost, Krissie had been sitting up straight, her eyes locked to the large window in front of her. Now she slouched dreadfully, her knees ached from sitting on them, and her head weighed heavily on her hands. Her eyes had become heavy from the weight of unshed tears, and she had finally determined to retreat to her room, when she happened to catch a glimpse of something out of the corner of her eye. At first she doubted her own eyesight, but as the figures approached she knew there could be no mistake.

"Maddy, Maddy!" Krissie yelled to her sister in the other room. "Mr. Fields has Scout! He's bringing him home to us!"

Maddy came charging into the living room, only to find the scene that Krissie had so perfectly described. She flung open the front door and ran outside with Krissie to welcome Scout home and thank their neighbor many times in succession.

"I found him in my garage," Mr. Fields explained. "He must have run in when my wife left for the grocery store. She came home a little while ago and found him sitting on the doorstep, longing to be let inside. The only trouble was it wasn't his house," he remarked smiling. He sensed what joy he was giving to his young neighbors, and he was delighted to have it in his gift.

"We can't thank you enough," Maddy assured her neighbor, as she received Scout's crudely constructed leash from his hand. Mr. Fields had found a piece of rope in his garage and attached it to Scout's collar in order to walk him home.

"It wasn't any trouble," Mr. Fields replied. "That's a good little dog you've got there. He didn't get into anything in the garage. I was surprised. My wife's cat is more trouble than that dog appears to be."

Maddy smiled, heaving a sigh of relief that seemed to come from her very core. She knew how curious Scout could be, and how much mischief he might do when he wanted to. She was thankful that everything had worked out so well at last. Scout was home safe and sound and he had not done damage to anything in Mr. Fields garage.

After Mr. Fields had turned to walk away, he looked back to see Krissie feeding Scout the plate of treats that Maddy had prepared.

"Looks like he's getting a welcome home celebration with all the fixings," the man hollered over his shoulder, greatly amused by the whole situation. Maddy and Krissie merely smiled in response. Ushering Scout inside after he had finished his meal, they sat down to relax for the first time in hours.

Kevin and Alex returned home not five minutes after Mr. Field's visit. They were ecstatic when they found Scout, or rather when he found them, at home. The little dog jumped for joy when he saw them, and acted as if the boys had been the ones missing instead of him.

Although it was past eight o' clock, Maddy and the others were finally able to enjoy dinner together. Maddy was sure the pizza would have been better fresh from the oven the first time, but she tried not to complain. After all, Scout was home safe.

Kevin volunteered to pray over their meal. He especially thanked God for Scout's safe arrival home. All were happy and light-hearted during dinner, except Maddy. She retreated to her room shortly after eating. Although she had intended to privately lament how the day had gone and how poorly she had managed everything, Kevin succeeded to spoil her plans. Maddy had made no effort to close the door to her room, feeling responsible not to block herself off from the others when she had been left in charge. This gave Kevin all the encouragement he needed. Rounding the corner into her room, he found Maddy sitting on her bed with her head in her hands, staring blankly into space.

"Knock, knock."

"Come on in," Maddy replied, without so much as a glance at her brother.

"No, no, no. You're supposed to say 'Who's there?' remember?" Kevin's comment at least caught Maddy's attention, but it was apparent she had not enjoyed the joke.

Determined to rescue Maddy from her own self-pity, Kevin pulled up a chair in front of her. "What's bothering you?" he asked, so directly that she had little opportunity for escape. Although she would have told him, Kevin could already guess what her trouble was. "You're thinking about what happened today, aren't you?"

Maddy heaved a little sigh. She knew Kevin could be stubborn when he wanted to be. She was sure he wouldn't leave her alone until she told him all.

"Yes, I was thinking about today," she admitted. "I was thinking about what might have happened to Scout and how I messed everything up."

While she was talking, Scout himself entered the room. As if on cue, he came and placed his paw on Maddy's knee. He had long since forgotten the slight Maddy had given him by forgetting him outside. His little stub tail wagged joyfully and his loving brown eyes stared at Maddy beneath his salt and pepper eyebrows.

"I'm sorry, Scout," Maddy apologized, while petting the little dog's head. "I'm sorry I forgot about you today. You might not have been lost so long, if only I had been paying closer attention."

Kevin remembered the main reason he had come to check on Maddy and told her that he and the others were going to watch a cartoon before heading to bed. He invited Maddy to join them.

"I'm past cartoons myself," Kevin informed Maddy as if the matter were somehow in question, "but I figure after the day we've all had it might be good to relax for a little while. Alex and Krissie argued over which tape to watch, but I worked out a compromise," Kevin said with satisfaction.

"Maybe Mom and Dad should have left you in charge," Maddy remarked passively, as she considered how well Kevin had handled the events of the day in comparison to her.

Kevin knew a merry heart was good medicine and he did what he could to "cure" his sister. "And leave me to make dinner?" he asked sarcastically. "Are you kidding? Even Scout probably wouldn't eat the food I'd fix," he continued, gesturing for Scout to come to him so he could scratch his favorite spot behind his ears.

For the first time since that awful moment of realization that she had been to blame for Scout's disappearance, Maddy felt at ease. She welcomed a time of relaxation before a good night's sleep, but rest did not easily come to the weary that night.

Four

Unwelcome Visitors

The antique grandfather clock in the living room had just finished tolling two o'clock. No one had awakened to its chimes, as they had all learned long before to sleep through them. Yet, no longer had the brass sound ceased, than other noises began to fill the air. The strange snarls and shrieks coming from right outside the girls' bedroom could not be so easily ignored. Scout's barks of warning began instantly, and soon Maddy and her siblings were all awake.

"What is that?" Krissie asked nervously, leaning over the edge of her bunk bed to peer down at her sister. Maddy was just waking up; she was still trying to establish fiction from reality since the episode had startled her out of a pleasant dream. Maddy could hear the noises for herself now and her heart began racing. As she started to reply to Krissie's question, Maddy felt and saw a beam of light shining upon her. She screamed instantly, then began to fear that she had endangered herself and her sister by her instinctive reaction.

Maddy breathed a sigh of relief as she became aware of her intruder's identity. Alex held the flashlight he had been carrying under his chin so that she could see him more clearly. Although his shadow made him appear considerably taller, Maddy could now recognize how Alex measured up to it.

"It's just me," he declared. Even in the dark, Maddy could see his expression. He may not have scared her intentionally, but Maddy could tell that he had enjoyed it in any case. Repulsed by the satisfaction he derived at her expense, Maddy hurled her pillow across the room at her younger brother.

"Don't ever do that to me again," she warned Alex ominously. Although Alex was preparing a speech in his own defense, Kevin, who had just come to stand behind him, put his hand on his brother's shoulder to quiet him. Now that they were all together in one room, the four turned their attention to what had caused them to awaken in the first place. They were silent, trying to discern the source of the strange sounds they heard. Scout did not lower his voice, however, and it was difficult to pay close attention to noises originating outside.

Now that Maddy felt safe to do so, she jumped out of bed to look out her front window. There in the moonlight she could see two raccoons scrapping with one another. She was not sure at first what it was they were fighting over, but the answer quickly came to her.

"Krissie, did you pick up the dog biscuits you put in the front yard for Scout to find when he was lost?" Maddy asked in order to verify her suspicions. She turned to see Krissie still hanging over the side of her bed with a wrinkled expression on her face.

"No," the little girl responded, her anxiety causing her to lisp, "was I suppothed to?" Maddy began laughing. After the day and night she had experienced, she felt half-mad. Krissie was relieved that her sister had not seen anything frightening outside, but she couldn't understand what was so comical about the situation.

"What's so funny?" she asked. Maddy told Krissie and her brothers that some raccoons had found Scout's biscuits in the front yard and were fighting over them.

"No wonder Scout's so angry," Alex remarked good-humoredly, "they're eating his biscuits!" His comment served to remind Maddy of the little dog who was still standing by the front door, barking ferociously. Maddy went to fetch him and tell him to quiet down. When she approached him, however, he edged closer to the front door, practically begging to tell the raccoons how he felt about them.

"No, not tonight," Maddy told Scout, who looked back at her with confusion apparent in his brown eyes. Scout did not know that Maddy had been left in charge of the household. He felt it was his duty to protect the family against all enemies, domesticated and non-domesticated. Still, he enjoyed the petting Maddy gave him. He would have to chase the raccoons another night.

When Maddy returned to her room, she found that Kevin and Alex had already gone back to bed. Maddy tiptoed quietly up to her bed, hoping not to disturb Krissie in case she had already fallen asleep. Krissie was not asleep, however, as Maddy soon discovered.

"Maddy," Krissie whispered, as she peeped her head out over the top bunk once again. Maddy had already become comfortable and made no effort to move in order to view her sister more clearly. She spoke without even opening her eyes.

"Yes, Krissie, what is it?" The tone of her voice showed the lack of enthusiasm she felt for further discussion this night.

"I'm really excited about tomorrow!" Krissie replied, her animation clearly making up for her sister's lack of it.

"Why's…that?" Maddy asked, yawning in between the two words.

"I'll have all sorts of stories about today to tell in Sunday school!" Krissie answered back.

Five

Home Sweet Home

"Well, here we are," Jared told Molly as he stopped the car in front of their military home. Molly could not help but recognize the surge of disappointment that rose in her breast as she looked at the small duplex building. While she had previously looked forward to setting up a home, no matter how humble, for Jared and herself, she now thought of how little it would mean once he had left for Iraq. This home before her might seem cozy and comfortable when Jared was there to share it with her, but Molly predicted it would likely feel small and sterile to her once she became its sole occupant. After all she had told herself about sacrifice and the service she would be doing to her country by supporting her husband on his mission, Molly now found herself selfishly wishing that Jared's occupation were different and that their adjustment to home life together would not be so soon interrupted.

While Molly had known that their honeymoon would not last forever, she now realized more fully what going home would mean. Jared would be returning to work. As the time of his deployment neared, he would become increasingly busy.

"Did you hear me?" Jared asked, causing Molly to momentarily put away her anxious thoughts.

"Yeah, I heard," Molly replied, hoping to appear more enthusiastic than she really felt.

"Are you okay? You seem a little depressed," Jared observed. On hearing Jared's comment, Molly knew she must try harder to appear brave.

"I'm all right, Jared," she replied. Changing the subject, she added, "We're home!"

After each had grabbed a small suitcase out of the trunk, Jared and Molly walked hand in hand toward their home. Molly's mind was still troubled, however, and she had no idea why, after reaching the front step, Jared had failed to open the door.

"Don't you have your key?" she asked him, a little frustrated.

"Yes, I have the key," Jared replied nonchalantly.

"Well?" Molly probed. She watched Jared unlock the door. As she started to head inside with her luggage, Jared stopped her. In a moment, her bag was on the ground and Molly found herself caught up in Jared's strong arms. Molly laughed at her own blindness in understanding her husband's intentions.

"What are you doing?" she asked him, even though she already knew the answer.

"I'm carrying you over the threshold, my fair princess," he responded, trying to appear serious, but smiling uncontrollably. "I know it's not a very becoming threshold, but just imagine we're standing in the doorway of some great castle in Europe." Molly began laughing again, this time at the contrast between what Jared was dreaming up and reality.

"Aren't you going to put me down now?" Molly asked, after they had been inside for a few moments.

"Not until milady gives me a kiss," he explained, his voice still hinged with humor. When Molly had done so, Jared let her gingerly down to the floor beneath. When she turned away from him with the intention of putting her things in order, however, Jared put his hands on her shoulders to stop her. He turned her around to face him, and she could tell his mood was different now. He wanted to confront the dark cloud that had been hanging over Molly since their arrival home.

"Hey," he said softly, trying to get Molly to look him in the eyes. She did her best to avoid his gaze, knowing what the outcome would be if she failed. When she finally looked up, Jared could see tears twinkling in her eyes.

"What's wrong?" he asked in concern. After Molly made no answer he ventured a guess. "This has something to do with me going away, doesn't it?" Molly nodded in response. She did not wish to speak, lest she make Jared too uneasy about her. She was satisfied that he understood how she felt and would have changed the subject if only Jared had allowed her to.

"I know how you must be feeling, Molly," he said. "I'll miss you so much. But do you remember the conversation we had, before we were even engaged?"

"Yes," she admitted meekly. Although she knew the point Jared was trying to make, she also considered that he had not chosen the strongest proof for his argument. "It seemed easy to accept things then because you were only in the military at that time. We weren't sure you'd be going overseas."

"True enough, but don't you remember how we both accepted that wherever God led us we would go? Right now, He's leading me overseas, but He won't leave me when I get there." Jared stopped to collect his thoughts and take hold of Molly's hands. If nothing else told of his wife's uneasiness, her fidgeting did. Although she remained silent, Molly had been actively playing with the rings on her fingers. It gave her something to focus on, no matter how trivial, other than the difficult conversation she and Jared were having. Now left to no distractions other than her own thoughts, however, Molly locked her gaze with Jared's. "God is always beside me in whatever I do," he continued. "He'll be with you too. Our relationship is built on something greater than ourselves, remember?"

Molly nodded her head once again. For a moment she felt speechless as she considered Jared's words and apparent composure. At last she admitted, “I don’t know how you can think to say things like that on the spot.”

“That’s because I didn’t,” Jared answered directly. The steadfast look in his blue eyes testified to the truth in what he had said, but Molly was intrigued to know more. She waited for him to continue, which he did after several moments had passed. “I’ve been saying these things to myself ever since I found out I’d be deployed.” Pausing again, Jared struggled to look into his wife’s eyes long enough to add, “And I’ll be saying them until I’m safely home again in your arms.”

In an instant, roles were reversed and Molly found herself comforting the one who had not long before sought to comfort her. As she held Jared’s head against her chest and tried to wipe away the tears that were running down his cheeks, Molly learned that she was not the only one who had been trying to appear brave.

Although Molly had grown up knowing nearly all her close neighbors, she failed to continue this custom in her new military community. She quickly found her days to be full between setting up her home and caring for Jared. While she knew it would be essential to find at least a few close friends in her new hometown, Molly imagined she would find them at church rather than among her neighbors. Since arriving home, Jared and Molly had been attending different churches, and it wasn’t long before they felt at home among a family of local believers. In a matter of weeks, Molly was looking to become involved in a women’s Bible study and volunteering to help in the church nursery. Whatever need Molly had for female companionship seemed to be filled by the interactions she had with the women at church. Being a young bride, Molly was especially grateful for the expertise of the older women, who gave her the seasoned encouragement and instruction she might have easily sought from her mother had she lived nearer.

Since Molly had not considered making much of an attempt of getting to know those living near her, it made the surprise even greater when one of her neighbors came to pay a call. Molly had been in the midst of unpacking boxes and moving small pieces of furniture one afternoon when she heard the doorbell ring. She knew that it was too early for Jared to be home. Opening the door hesitantly, Molly spied a young woman standing on her doorstep with a covered dish in her hands. She happened to be looking off in another direction at that particular moment, and Molly had the opportunity to steal the first first impression. Molly was not sure of the woman's age, but she appeared to be in her mid-twenties. Her vibrant red hair was cut a few inches below her ears, and she had it tucked neatly behind them, with a single barrette holding the section into which more of her hair had been parted. Molly could make out from her profile that the woman had a faint array of freckles scattered across her face. She was dressed for the warm summer day, wearing a turquoise tank top, tan khaki shorts, and a pair of decorative flip- flops. Although Molly might have surveyed her visitor more without her awareness, a creak in the door caused by its increased opening caught the young woman's attention. She whirled around and with a broad smile showing over remarkably white teeth, reached out a hand and introduced herself.

"Hi, I'm Heather Banks," she began in a slightly more high-pitched tone of voice than what Molly was used to hearing, but which she soon learned to be natural, not assumed. "My husband and I have seen you and your husband around, but we haven't taken the time to stop by yet. I didn't want to wait any longer, even though Terry wasn't able to come with me." Molly was pleasantly surprised by Heather's introduction, and only wished that she had been friendlier herself. Heather's warm manner made Molly comfortable about inviting her inside, though she still found herself apologizing for the current state of disarray in which the living room was.

"Oh, please, don't apologize," Heather answered abruptly. "Terry and I must be some of the slowest un-packers there ever were! We joke that we might as well live out of our boxes, since it seems that by the time we unpack them it's time to transfer to our new station."

A sudden thought struck Molly, and she couldn't help satisfying her curiosity. "Do you know long you and your husband will be stationed here?" she asked. Even though she had just met Heather, she seemed to be the sort of person that Molly might love to call a close friend. She knew that it was necessary in the military to make fast friends, but she still longed to have some long-term friendships if it were possible.

"We've only been here for about three months. We don't foresee being called to move anytime in the next two years or so," Heather said easily enough. Molly's heart was jubilant at the prospect of a friend living next door, yet it still pondered the almost characteristic indifference so many people in the Air Force had to living wherever they were beckoned to call home. She had been exceedingly grateful when Jared was able to secure a position at a base only five hours from her hometown. She knew that she would get used to frequent transfers in time, but her current situation required enough adjustment in itself that she wondered if a different assignment might not have fully taxed her strength.

Molly's mind was called away from her reflections by Heather's next string of conversation.

"Isn't it funny how you carry things around and forget what you're doing with them?" she asked rhetorically, not pausing long enough to let Molly make any attempt at an answer. "I've been holding these cookies without offering them to you." As she said this much, Heather held out the plate in her hands. Molly took them as they were offered and replied that she and Jared would surely enjoy them.

"How long have you been married?" Heather inquired. Her question made Molly faintly blush as she knew the answer she must give would illicit her friend's curiosity.

"Just a few weeks," she admitted, her eyebrows contracting slightly as she did. Molly watched Heather's expression quickly turn soft and sentimental. Apparently,

Heather too was a romantic. It was just one more thing that Molly could add to the rapidly growing list of qualities she liked about her.

"That's so sweet," Heather replied simply, before reminiscing a little herself. "Terry and I just exited the newlywed stage of our relationship. It's hard to believe that it's been two years already." Although she had said her last words almost to herself, she addressed her next comment directly to Molly, "My best advice is just to enjoy each day as it comes. They all pass away soon enough." Molly smiled with an inward knowledge that Heather's words were true, no matter how difficult their application might seem to be. She had been wrestling daily with this very issue ever since returning from her honeymoon. It was always good, Molly thought, to have someone else reinforce a lesson she was trying to teach herself. Still, Molly wondered if Heather could know the anxiety she felt concerning Jared's upcoming deployment. Had Heather's husband ever been sent overseas? If so, had she been able to live up to her own advice?

As Molly pondered these things, Heather interrupted her thoughts to say that she needed to head home to start fixing dinner. Apparently Heather worked during the morning and early afternoon. She had only been home long enough to change clothes, fix cookies, and pay a short visit to Molly. Recognizing how she had made stopping by a priority, Molly sincerely thanked Heather for her thoughtfulness. She assured her she was welcome to come by any day, and told her that she hoped she could soon meet Jared. Heather seemed to brush off any thanks, but welcomed the idea of more visits with Molly and her husband. She left as thoroughly pleased with her new neighbor as Molly had been.

Six

Leaving

As the weeks progressed, Jared and Molly became better acquainted with Heather and her husband, Terry. Terry Banks was nearly as outgoing as his wife and had nine years' experience in the Air Force, having joined right out of high school. Jared generally enjoyed listening to him recount his various adventures and misadventures in the military. He only hoped his memory would preserve Terry's valuable advice and not the strong language that was frequently used in giving it.

Once she learned of the time Heather and Terry had spent in Germany, Molly was anxious to hear as much about their travels as she could. Molly's maternal grandmother had lived in Germany as a child and had always been full of stories for Molly anytime she used to visit. Somehow this link made Molly feel closer to Heather, yet she was sadly disappointed to learn that, whatever other things they might have in common, Molly could not regard Heather as a sister in Christ. It was a wonder to her how some people without true peace and joy could seem to possess the qualities, while others appeared to lack them, even though they had claim to them.

Molly had been hopeful for her friend's spiritual condition, until one day a few weeks into their acquaintance Heather openly declared what she thought about God. The two had been discussing Jared's upcoming deployment and Heather had told Molly how much she admired her bravery.

"I don't know what I'd do if I were you, Molly. I'd be worried about Terry every moment he was gone."

"You mean Terry's never been sent on a similar mission before?" Molly asked, anxious to shift the focus off herself. She was glad she had at least been able to *appear* brave. She only wished she could manage as well around Jared as she seemed to around Heather.

"Oh, he's been to some different places in Europe besides our tour in Germany, but never the Middle East. We've been lucky I guess. I can't imagine what I'd do if he were sent some place really dangerous." Heather stopped herself then, but she knew she had already planted the thought in Molly's mind. She apologized instantly and was more than surprised by Molly's calm response.

"The way I see it, he's really in no more danger in Iraq than he is in Illinois." *At least, that's what I keep saying to myself,* Molly added inwardly. When Heather did not respond, Molly looked back at her friend. She appeared perplexed to say the least, the crinkle in her light red eyebrows still visible. Molly wished she could know what she was thinking. After all, her words had not been revolutionary.

Aware of her friend's close inspection of her, Heather shrugged her shoulders awkwardly, forcing a half-hearted smile. It appeared she had no wish to discourage Molly from a belief that gave her comfort, no matter how incredible she considered it to be.

"It's not something I can readily believe myself," Molly continued, hoping that Heather's reaction might improve once she had explained herself further, "but that's where I have to have faith." As Molly finished her sentence, Heather shifted a little uncomfortably in her seat. Although Molly noticed her movement immediately, she meant to finish saying what was on her heart. "All Jared's days, and mine, were written in God's book before we were even born." *I keep saying this to myself because I need to hear it, but maybe Heather needs to hear it more!* Molly thought, glad she had not been inclined to stop speaking by Heather's apparent discomfort.

Again, Heather had nothing to say, and could only smile in response. Molly thought her look was one of a mother gently listening to her child speak of his make-believe friend.

"Don't you believe in God?" Molly asked suddenly, clinging to a thread of hope that she had misjudged her friend. Heather's struggle for words and those she eventually chose, however, told Molly that her perception had been accurate. Heather believed in *a god*, but not in the God that Molly knew. "Someone had to get the ball rolling," she said, but just who that was or what he was like was beyond her. Besides, it didn't matter what one believed anyway, since whoever created the world didn't seem to have any dealings in it anymore.

As Molly listened to her friend, her heart ached for her. Instantly, she began searching for words to say, only to be interrupted by Heather's apology that she had already stayed too late and needed to head back home. Molly tried to be gracious about her sudden departure, even though she felt it was just an excuse to terminate their conversation.

Stepping out the front door, Heather promised, with her usual cheerfulness, to have Molly over to her home sometime.

"I'll look forward to it!" Molly answered enthusiastically. *Maybe we can talk some more then,* she said to herself.

It wasn't like Molly to wake up before her alarm clock went off. Usually it took the device's loud rhythmic beeping in her ears to bring her to a consciousness of the new day. Even then Molly often struggled to coax her body out of bed. One morning, however, she found herself awake without any extraneous aid. Rolling over to check the time, Molly grimaced to see it was not yet five. Knowing there would be no point in getting back to sleep now, she rubbed her eyes and stretched her arms above her head, being careful not to disturb her still sleeping husband.

As she became increasingly aware of the new day, Molly recognized that she did not feel herself. Although she could not remember the details of any of her dreams, she thought for sure they must have been more like nightmares, since she woke up with a queer sort of anxiety. Her stomach too seemed uneasy and she almost felt she might become sick. Then, as if the day had dawned upon her, Molly remembered, and any physical discomfort she felt was temporarily forgotten. *Jared is leaving today*. The day that both had tried valiantly not to worry or think about had come at last. No wonder Molly felt so horrible.

Instead of lying in bed and feeling powerless, Molly decided to prepare herself mentally and physically for the day ahead. Jared would be up in half-an-hour and Molly hoped to have his breakfast going by the time he awoke.

Quietly grabbing her robe from the closet, Molly tiptoed to the bathroom. She was abruptly stopped, however, by a sudden dizzy spell that almost sent her reeling to the floor. Steadying herself against the wall, she spent a few moments trying to regain her balance. Recognizing today more than ever how much she needed to rest in the Lord, Molly took advantage of the opportunity to silently pray.

"Lord, I don't know how I'm going to get through this today. I feel miserable, inside and out. I know Jared was right when he said You would always be with us. Please be with us today, Father. Help Jared to bear it and help me to support him and not cause him more pain than he's already experiencing. Please keep him and the others safe. In Jesus' name, Amen." Molly opened her eyes and heaved a little sigh. She could do no more to help the situation than she had just done. It was in God's hands. Just as she could lean against a wall to steady her weary self, she could rely on God to give peace and rest to her troubled heart.

Molly had just finished cooking Jared's eggs when he came sauntering into the kitchen. Although he had done his best to keep his anxiety from showing through his facial expressions,

Jared's slow-paced strides and slouched shoulders gave testimony to his struggle.

"Good morning, Sweetie," he said, coming up beside Molly to place a kiss on her cheek. "You're up awfully early." Even Molly's morning routine drew attention to the fact that this day was unlike any other. Although she had not planned it this way, Molly knew that by being up early enough to fix Jared's breakfast, she was adding significance to the day. Jared generally had to help himself to dry cereal in the mornings. While he might have enjoyed the special attention under normal circumstances, today it seemed another difficult reminder of his deployment. Even Molly began to wish she had found another use for the extra time she had this morning.

"Yeah, well, I woke up before the alarm went off and I thought I would get your breakfast started," she replied easily enough. Jared studied Molly as she set the table for one and sat down.

"Aren't you going to join me?" he asked.

"I'll sit with you, of course, but honestly I couldn't eat anything. I feel a little sick this morning." Jared's gaze fell at Molly's admission; he could guess why she was feeling poorly. He wished he could do something to ease the pain of separation, but it could not be helped. As Jared reached out his hand and placed it on Molly's, he looked up into her hazel eyes. Allowing his gaze to linger for a moment, Jared tried to read his wife's thoughts through her careworn expression. Meanwhile, Molly, who was used to Jared placing his hand on hers before prayer, wondered at his silence.

"Aren't you going to pray?" she asked him. "Your eggs are getting cold."

Jared was glad that Molly had not noticed him studying her and appreciated her mention of prayer. It would ease his mind this of all mornings just to remember that God was in control. Still, he refrained from saying anything in his prayer that might give Molly more cause for concern.

The next hour was swallowed up in Jared's preparations for the day. Molly felt numb as she watched her husband go through his morning routine in the usual fashion. Except for the packed items by the front door, nothing in the house hinted that the day was different from any others. For a fleeting moment Molly asked herself if Jared's deployment weren't merely a bad dream like the one she had had that night. How she wished to awaken from it all, to find Jared returning to her at the end of the day!

A few minutes later Molly heard a car door close and she rushed to the window. *They're here*, she said to herself before alerting Jared. Soon all the bags were packed and Jared was left alone with Molly for one last goodbye.

Holding his wife close to his chest, Jared absently stroked Molly's long hair. His mind was absorbed in a search for something to say. Although he'd given this moment a great deal of thought before, he couldn't seem to choke out any of the speeches he had prepared. In the end, he could only assure Molly of his ardent love for her and that she would be continually in his prayers. One last long kiss goodbye and *he was gone*.

Seven

Discoveries

No matter how she tried, Molly could not seem to regain her strength or rally her spirits during the first few weeks after Jared's departure. Although she knew she would have to get used to living by herself for the time being, Molly was unable to shake the physical or emotional depression that had taken hold of her. Most mornings she woke up feeling nauseous, and her desire to settle her stomach with a little breakfast was the most motivating factor she had for getting out of bed. At first, she attributed every symptom she experienced to the far-reaching effects of Jared's deployment. It did not even cross her mind to consider other alternatives. If only she were stronger and more able to bear up under the pressures of life, she might feel better.

Yet, as her complaints mounted up, Molly began to consider another possibility. Perhaps there was nothing wrong with her after all. At first the thought seemed too wonderful to be true, but the very next day her spirits soared with the knowledge of the new life inside her.

As unromantic as it was, Molly sent Jared an e-mail that afternoon to let him know he would soon become a father. She tried wording the news a number of ways, before throwing her hands up in frustration. As thankful as she was for the opportunity to instantly communicate with her husband half-way around the world, it was no substitute for actual conversation.

What she wouldn't give to see the look on Jared's face when he read her e-mail! No, she could only imagine his expression, even if she felt pretty sure her picture wasn't far from the truth.

Molly's family was nearly as excited as Molly herself when she told them the good news that evening. Helen was in raptures, not only to find she would become a grandmother in a matter of months, but also to know that Molly would now have something else to distract her attention while Jared was away. She knew she worried too much about her daughter who had only recently left home. She wished more than ever that she could be close to her now, but she trusted that Molly would take good care of herself and the baby.

Molly's brothers and sisters were especially proud to think of themselves as aunts and uncles, although the thought of Krissie being an aunt at eight years of age made them all laugh. A few days later, Maddy was still thinking about her coming niece or nephew as she sat next to her good friend, Wesley, in the bleachers of their county fairgrounds, waiting for the motor cross show to start. Although she had been talking on her new favorite subject for a full ten minutes, Maddy soon realized that Wesley had not been engaged in the conversation.

"Have you thought about who you'll go with to homecoming this year?" Wesley asked suddenly, before reaching up to brush a strand of his thick sandy brown hair out of his eye. No matter how he tried, Wesley was never able to tame the cowlick that caused a small section of his long hair to frequently obstruct his vision. Although Wesley's distracting movement gave Maddy a second to collect her thoughts, it was far from enough for her to feel at ease about making any sort of reply. Wesley had introduced the subject without any prior warning and it had caught her completely off guard.

"Homecoming?" she asked incredulously. "Our senior year hasn't even started yet!"

"So," Wesley uttered in response, shrugging his shoulders, "we'll be getting our senior pictures done next month and we won't be graduating till June. That's an even longer wait."

"That's different."

"I don't see how. Besides, you didn't answer my question." Although Wesley had formerly spoken as if merely trying to pass the time, his tone now turned serious. He even seemed a little irritated that Maddy had not considered the subject before.

"Well, if you know I think it's too early to think about homecoming, then you also should know I haven't thought of who I'm going with." Maddy wondered what had caused Wesley to mention homecoming in the first place. She was enjoying the summer too fully to be thinking about social arrangements she would make once returning to school.

"Would you go with me?" Wesley asked, with a little hesitation apparent in his voice. Wesley was rarely serious about anything in Maddy's presence. As she read his gaze, Maddy began to feel a little uneasy about responding. Why did his green eyes look so strange, as if their depths held more than they wished to express? Although Maddy could not keep the thought from suggesting itself to her mind that Wesley had begun to care for her as more than the friend she had been to him for almost ten years, she wouldn't allow herself to consider it seriously. Wesley had known her from childhood; he was aware of all her quirks and habits. She had not changed much; in many ways, she still resembled the young girl who had begged to play soccer with him and the other boys after school. If she wasn't that different, then surely Wesley's feelings for her couldn't have altered so entirely. When at last Maddy gave her answer, it was accompanied by her focused determination not to read anything into Wesley's words beyond their literal meaning.

"Well, sure," she replied cautiously and at length. "We went together last year and had a good time. I don't see why we couldn't this year too." *There,* Maddy thought to herself, *he can hardly get excited about that response.* How Wesley took her words, she wasn't sure. All Maddy knew was that Wesley's mind had momentarily drifted miles away since he had to ask her to repeat the next words she spoke.

“I said that although we’ve figured this out, we’ll still have to wait a few months,” Maddy repeated. “Homecoming isn’t until October.”

Hearing the clock chime seven o’clock, Molly started to clean up her half-eaten dinner. There was no need to be in any hurry, but she felt it would be better to keep on some sort of schedule. This evening she had been more interested in the book she was reading than her soup. Maybe after she had put a few dishes away she could curl up on the couch and read a few more chapters.

Although it had appeared promising, Molly’s plan didn’t work out as she had hoped. Somehow her mind kept trailing off. How could she indulge in the comfort and safety of her home knowing that Jared was overseas working hard in one the world’s greatest hot spots? Yet, what else could she do?

Turning toward the back of the couch so she could bury her face in the pillows, Molly allowed herself to cry. She had tried to be brave, but wondered how much more she could endure. If only Jared could be there to comfort her, even for a moment. Molly’s mind was so far away that it failed to register the first few rings of the telephone that began a minute later. Suddenly, she jumped up and ran to grab the receiver. She wished she didn’t always have a sense of dread every time the phone rang, and she let out a sigh of relief when she heard Heather’s greeting across the line.

“Are you okay, Molly?” Heather asked with apparent concern, after hearing Molly's sniffles in the background.

“Well, actually, I’ve not had the greatest day today,” was Molly’s honest reply. Heather easily guessed that her friend’s response had been a mild one. Molly was surely feeling worse than she let on.

"Do you want some company?" Heather's words beckoned to Molly like a light to a ship lost in the waves of the sea.

"I would love some!" Molly was already anticipating her friend's visit when she considered she might have been too eager to accept her offer. "That is, if you can spare the time. Terry won't mind, will he?"

"Oh, no," Heather said good-naturedly. "He actually abandoned me tonight. He's out with some friends of his who are in town. No, to tell you the truth, I was just here washing some dishes when I felt the sudden urge to call you. Isn't it funny how these things work out?"

Molly smiled and sighed as she listened to Heather's reply. *She* knew it was no coincidence that Heather had called when she did. It was ironic to Molly that Heather, who believed in the existence of God yet didn't think He had anything to do with everyday life, had just been used by Him in a very personal way.

"I'll be over in five minutes," Heather told her friend.

Eight

Coming Home after Homecoming

Maddy watched as Wesley's car backed out of her driveway and onto the quiet street. Even in the moonlight Maddy could see the sullen look on Wesley's face. It was the same face that had looked at her so earnestly just an hour before, when Wesley had revealed to Maddy how much he cared for her. As she turned to go inside the house, Maddy brushed aside the tears that trickled down her cheeks. She wished she could so easily brush aside the pain and regret she felt.

Helen had been waiting up for her daughter. While she trusted both Wesley and Maddy, she found that she never could sleep when her children were out late. She did not want to worry, so she spent the silent hours reading a book. It took her mind off the situation and, with all the others in bed, she relished the rare opportunity to spend some quiet time alone.

Hearing the door knob turn, Helen laid aside her book and her reading glasses. She watched Maddy as she entered the house and closed the door behind her. Helen said nothing, yet her eyes seemed to ask for her how the evening had gone. She was surprised and distressed when Maddy did not respond, but fled to her mother's side for comfort.

"What is it?" Helen asked her distraught daughter. "What happened, Maddy?" It was a minute before Maddy could gather strength enough to talk. In that minute, Helen thought of all the things that might have happened to make Maddy so upset.

Absent from her list of suspicions was the truth that Maddy finally managed to choke out in between sobs.

"Wesley…told me…that he…loved me tonight."

Every indicator told Helen that Maddy did not desire Wesley's love the way he meant it, and it did not surprise her. Maddy and Wesley had been friends since childhood. Maddy never seemed to have many girlfriends, although she and Molly had always been close, despite the differences in their ages. When they were young it had seemed natural for Maddy and Wesley to spend time together. They had shared a lot of the same interests and were only a week apart in age. Yet, Maddy and Wesley were not children anymore. Glancing down at her daughter, Helen remembered thinking how grown up Maddy had looked to her eyes just hours before, with her light red hair pulled up in an elegant twist and gently cascading ringlets framing her face. Although the loose-fitting, casual attire Maddy usually wore failed to flatter her tall, lean figure, the hunter green dress she had chosen for this evening made her appear distinctively feminine and sophisticated. Remembering how her daughter's face had radiated with lovely animation and excitement just a short time ago, Helen ached to see how quickly her dreams had been dashed. Although her strongest wish was that she could somehow put the situation to rights, Helen knew that this sort of disillusionment was something that her daughter would continue to face if she were ever to experience the mixed blessing of being an adult.

"And this is upsetting you, I take it," she quietly affirmed after some moments had passed.

"Yes," Maddy whispered, slowly regaining her composure. "I guess I didn't really see it coming. I only ever saw Wesley as a friend. Not just a friend, my best friend. Now that's gone forever. Now I have no one." As Maddy broke out into a fresh flow of tears, Helen considered how unfortunate the timing of this situation had been, since Maddy had just lost her sister as a close confidante. Still, she thought that a little dose of perspective might offer some hope.

"How do you know that it's over forever?" Helen asked, while gently stroking her daughter's hair. Maddy could not see her mother's eyes, since her head was positioned against her shoulder; however, she could imagine them gleaming with the hope that seemed to flow within Helen like a spring. Maddy listened patiently, but she could not picture things ever being the same as they had been.

"You don't know how he looked at me, Mom," Maddy admitted. "For a minute I wanted to fall off the face of the earth." *I've always wanted a guy to look at me that way,* Maddy thought to herself, *but not Wesley*!

"I was so excited about this year," she continued, as if Helen had not already known her daughter's anticipations for her senior year of high school. "There are going to be so many things going on, and now my best friend won't be there to share them with me. Everyone is supposed to enjoy their senior year."

"Says who?" Helen asked lightheartedly. Startled by her mother's unforeseen question, Maddy sat up straight in order to read her face. As she did so, her lips couldn't help giving a small semblance of a smile. How was it that her mother could so often manage to see things in a different light than the rest of the world? Maddy had seen her on numerous occasions take charge of circumstances that would have otherwise taken charge of her. Although a part of her didn't want to heed any voice of reason, Maddy managed to resist it and take comfort in her mother's words.

"You're smart enough to know that what's inside the packaging isn't often as good as what's on the label," Helen continued in explanation. Smiling, she added, "Besides, this just might be a blessing in disguise." Although her heart was not fully convinced of her mother's last statement, Maddy leaned over to give Helen a hug.

"Thanks, Mom," she whispered in her ear. Sitting back to brush away some of the tears that continued to blur her vision, she added, "And thanks for waiting up for me. I don't know what I would have done if there had been no one for me to talk to."

"Me? I was reading a book, remember?" was Helen's half-way honest reply. No matter how her mother sought to hide it, Maddy knew Helen's real reason for staying up late. She was a concerned mother, but she had no cause to tell Maddy so. It showed through, in spite of everything.

"Why don't you get some sleep, hmm?" Helen suggested, breaking the peaceful silence that had just settled in the living room like a light fog in the midst of a valley. Although her heart was still heavy, Maddy did not resist the idea of sleep. Characteristically remarking that she would be glad to remove her make-up and all the bobby pins that had been poking at the back of her scalp throughout the evening, she made her way to her room.

Helen's eyes followed Maddy until she disappeared out of sight. What she felt was a mixture of sympathy and relief. Helen understood Maddy's disappointment over the anticipated loss of her best friend. However, she also breathed a sigh of relief that Maddy would not be too soon in following her sister to the altar. *After all*, she remembered, *Jared and Molly were high school sweethearts*.

Nine

An Unexpected Arrival

"Tammy, quit pushing Annie," Helen commanded, frustration wearing through her ordinarily cheerful voice. "There's enough room for everyone." Helen ran a hand through her blond-gray hair to tame the strand that just fallen in her face. She knew that in just a little over two weeks the group of children before her would stage their Christmas program. Two weeks, and yet the stage was still in the drafting process! Two weeks, and yet the children seemed more intent on playing or bickering amongst themselves than performing!

Helen reached for her water bottle and took a sip of cool water, giving her mind a moment to reassess how she might get a handle on herself and the situation. After failing to think of any better alternatives, Helen returned to the task at hand, only to be interrupted by the sound of footsteps behind her. Turning around, she saw Charlotte Sanders coming to meet her. As the children recognized the lady who had been a Sunday school teacher for many of them, they began chanting, "Miss Charlotte! Miss Charlotte!" A few children even left their places on the stage to run down and see her. Krissie was one of them, and the look she soon received from her mother warned her that she would be hearing about her action once at home. Krissie thought to herself, while returning to her place on the stage, that her mother's look was truly punishment enough.

If Helen had felt the children were out of control before, they were only worse after Charlotte's arrival. Helen was not sure why Charlotte had come to see her, and she tried to check the hostilities growing inside her. She had had a hard enough time trying to discipline the children before; now she estimated it would be a good ten minutes before they would be sufficiently calmed down to make any progress. Charlotte was considered a favorite by many of the children, and by appearing at their choir practice, she had given even the more docile boys and girls a good reason to become excited.

"Did you come to hear us sing, Miss Charlotte?" asked Lexi, an ordinarily quiet and soft-spoken six-year-old. Charlotte replied that this had been part of her reason for coming. *What other reason is there?* Helen thought to herself. Charlotte had not spoken to Helen before about attending the children's choir rehearsal and, as yet, she had failed to give any reason for her appearance. Although Helen had not expected her to stay for any length of time, Charlotte was now removing her hat and gloves. While Helen hoped that Charlotte was just feeling particularly warm this evening, a growing conviction inside her said that Charlotte meant to stay.

"How are you doing this evening, Helen?" Charlotte asked in her usual sweet, slow manner of speaking. Her cheeks were still glowing from their exposure to the brisk December night air. Their blush only accentuated her naturally red hair, which had lost little of its splendor even though some strands were beginning to gray.

"Thank you, I'm doing..." Helen paused before finishing her sentence. She really felt weary and hopelessly outnumbered; however, she did not want to admit it to Charlotte. "I'm doing as well as can be expected," she said at length. After returning Charlotte's greeting and being informed that Charlotte was "wonderful", Helen inquired, "What brings you here tonight?" Many of the children were playing by themselves now, and Helen was watching them out of the corner of her eye to make sure no one became too wild.

"Well, I thought that you might be needing help with the children's Christmas program, so here I am." It took Charlotte much less time to explain herself than it did for Helen to comprehend her answer. As Charlotte looked down and began unbuttoning the large, round buttons of her pea-coat, Helen's mind overflowed with questions. *What made her assume I needed help? Why didn't she ask me first? How can I tell her I'm really doing okay? Is that even the truth?*

"How can I help you the most?" Charlotte's sudden question brought Helen back to reality. Glancing out of the corner of her eye how uncontrolled the children were becoming, Helen attempted to quiet them. Before the words were out of her mouth, however, Charlotte gently requested that they return to the stage and speak silently to each other. They seemed to follow her instructions blindly and Helen was embarrassed to think that this was the quietest the sanctuary had been all evening.

"Thank you, Charlotte. I know it doesn't look like it at the moment, but I really don't need the extra help." Helen doubted the accuracy of her words, but she was quick to give Charlotte the explanation she had been giving herself, "Maddy is usually here with me, but she had something going on with one of her friends tonight." Charlotte smiled sweetly in response and Helen could tell she remained unconvinced.

Charlotte had no children of her own; she had never married. She was a few years younger than Helen and, although the two seemed to have many things in common, they never spent much time together. Helen respected Charlotte for teaching one of the children's Sunday school classes for over ten years running. What she found hard to tolerate were some of Charlotte's methods of dealing with children. The way she seemed to bribe her pupils to be good by offering them treats often grated on Helen, who thought that good behavior was to be expected, not rewarded. Helen was sure that Charlotte was not stern enough when it came to discipline, since a few years before Krissie had told her mother that she had not been punished for acting up in class. As Helen remembered it, Krissie said that all Charlotte did was speak to her about her actions without denying her any privileges. And then there was the way that Charlotte asked a child if something was "okay", as if the choice was up to him or her.

Helen had been parenting for over twenty years, and she had seen the effectiveness of her methods. Yet, when she was truly honest with herself, she recognized that Charlotte's ways of dealing with children were also often successful. During the time that Krissie had spent in Charlotte's Sunday school class, she had learned nearly two dozen Bible verses by heart. Charlotte's influence with Krissie had been so great that, after advancing to the next class, Krissie would still head down the hall each week to visit her former teacher.

"Helen," Charlotte said gently after a few moments had passed, "I know what you're trying to do." Helen started at her words, but recognizing the softness of Charlotte's smile and voice, her fears quickly vanished. Charlotte had apparently not read the truth that Helen was used to handling the Christmas program her own way, and she secretly dreaded the thought of having to cooperate with another who would question her methods and step on her toes. Helen knew her attitude was not Christ-like, still, she did not feel the Christmas program would be a positive experience for anyone involved if she were forced to work with Charlotte.

"You feel that working with the kids would be a burden to me," Charlotte continued, trying to summarize what she thought was Helen's reservation. "I promise you it wouldn't be too much work for me. Being around children seems to give me energy rather than take it away." Charlotte's hazel eyes seemed to sparkle as she spoke. Helen opened her mouth to offer one more objection, but she could not get a single word out. She saw how important helping with this program was to Charlotte, and she did not have the heart to turn her away.

"Thank you," Helen replied at length. Faced with no other visible alternative, she resigned herself to making the best of the situation. Maybe Charlotte would content herself with simply helping the children on and off stage and memorizing their lines. Charlotte had asked how she could help the most, so Helen suggested that she concentrate on these two priorities.

Charlotte, however, was not one who could fully occupy herself with busywork. She soon began asking questions about the play, the characters, the set, the music, and more. She thought that they should have some of the girls act as angels as well as the boys.

"I remember when I was a child I got to play the part of an angel," Charlotte reminisced in Helen's hearing. "My mother made me the most beautiful wings. They sparkled more than the tinsel on a Christmas tree. All the other angels were envious, I think." Charlotte giggled as she spoke, but Helen merely smiled. It was a forced smile at that. Helen soon afterward told Charlotte why she had chosen to only give the roles to the boys in the choir.

"Whenever angels are spoken of in the Bible they are characteristically men," Helen informed her new assistant. "I know we often picture angels as girls, but there is not a Scriptural basis for it." Helen knew her words sounded more appropriate for one of her children than for a woman near her age; yet Charlotte's comments and curiosity tried her patience the same way a child's might.

Charlotte nodded her head in understanding and admitted that Helen "was probably right". Still, she continued to question Helen's judgment on other facets of the play.

When eight o'clock at last rolled around, Helen was thoroughly exhausted. Between working with the children and debating Charlotte on various points of the play, all she wanted to do was go home and get some rest. Helen found it strange that Charlotte should seem so relaxed and animated at the end of practice. Did children really give her the energy she said they did?

Helen was relieved the evening was over, yet her former anxieties returned when Charlotte said goodbye.

“I’ll see you next week,” she remarked cheerfully before exiting the choir room.

Ten

A Different Opinion

Helen was surprised to find Maddy at home when she returned from choir practice with Alex and Krissie. It was not quite eight-thirty, and Maddy had arranged to go Christmas shopping with her friend, Tara. Helen worried that her daughter had had a bad time, but Maddy quickly put her fears to rest.

"Tara had a headache, so we decided to go home early," she explained. Noticing the sullen looks on the faces of her siblings, Maddy smiled widely at her brother and sister and told them she had purchased their Christmas presents that evening. Just as Maddy anticipated, Alex and Krissie rapidly became animated and began asking, "What did you get me?" Maddy told them that they would find out on December 25th and not before. *Was I that impatient as a child?* she wondered to herself.

Shifting her gaze from her siblings to her mother, Maddy could tell that Helen looked tired and weary. She felt a twinge of guilt that she had not gone to help this evening. She knew the children could be particularly hard to control from time to time. Apparently this had been one of those times.

"How did it go, Mom?" Maddy asked gently. "Were the kids a handful tonight? I'm sorry I wasn't there to help. I can imagine it must have been overwhelming being the only one there." Before Helen could respond to Maddy's questions, Krissie interrupted to give her sister the news of the evening.

"Mommy wasn't the only teacher tonight," she explained enthusiastically. "Miss Charlotte came to help!" Maddy watched Krissie's face light up at the mention of her favorite teacher. Maddy had a warm spot in her heart for Charlotte too, having also been her pupil many years previous. Yet, as she looked up at her mother, Maddy could tell that Helen's feelings were quite different from Krissie's. She did not have time to analyze them further, however, as Helen told her two younger children to get ready for bed, then went to make preparations herself.

Helen was glad to have been spared answering Maddy's questions, but she didn't have the same good fortune with her husband. She had said little to him since returning home, hoping to avoid any explanations until the following day when she felt more composed. Timothy was on the last page of his book when Helen climbed into bed. Trying to avoid his gaze, she quickly bade him "good night" and snuggled under the sheets and comforter.

"Helen?" Timothy's voice seemed to betray more confusion than annoyance, but Helen still dreaded the conversation to come. Propping her pillow up so she could sit against it, Helen apologized for being quiet, but explained that she was thoroughly exhausted from the children's play practice. Timothy nodded understandingly, then launched into one of his usual direct questions.

"Was there one part of practice that was more exhausting than the others?" he asked, reaching for his wife's hand.

"Yes," Helen replied, trying to remain calm while her conversations with Charlotte flooded her memory. "Although I had not asked for more help, Charlotte Sanders came to volunteer her time to help with the Christmas pageant."

Timothy was already beginning to put the picture together in his mind. Although he knew Charlotte to be a tenderhearted Christian lady who had devoted many years of her life to working with children, his children included, her unrequested assistance must have strained Helen's already irritated nerves. After twenty-five years of marriage, Timothy had become well acquainted with his wife's strengths and weaknesses. Helen was a natural born leader, and her self-discipline had proved invaluable as a wife and mother. Yet, when it came to cooperating with others in a leadership role, Helen often struggled.

"Charlotte volunteered without your asking?" Timothy restated cautiously. "I wonder why. I'm sure she meant to be helpful."

"Maybe, but she wasn't. She criticized how I organized the play. She wanted to know why I hadn't included wise men or made any of the angels out to be girls." Remembering how slighted she had felt at the time, Helen let out a heavy sigh.

"Well, at least she is interested in the play and in helping you," Timothy offered as an alternative perspective.

"I don't need her kind of help," was Helen's decided answer.

"How do you know you don't?" Timothy's eyes searched his wife's face. Although he understood Helen's frustration, he also hoped she might see beyond her own expectations and consider the blessing it might be to Charlotte to be allowed to help with the play. Before another word could pass his lips, however, Helen interjected.

"Because it's not really help!" she exclaimed, her voice beginning to sound strained. "She only slowed me down today with all her comments." As tired as Helen had been when she arrived home, she could not think of sleeping now. All she wanted to do was prove to her husband that she was justified in her feelings and he had no right to question her anymore.

"Tonight was her first night helping," Timothy spoke as a gentle reminder. "Charlotte might have just needed someone to talk to. She doesn't have her own family, remember. She volunteers a lot of her time to the church." Helen had begun to feel a twinge of guilt when Timothy made mention of Charlotte's situation in life, but it quickly vanished with the subject of volunteering.

"What do you think I'm doing?" she asked hastily, pulling her hand out of Timothy's in order to fold her arms across her chest. "I have a family *and* I'm volunteering!"

"It isn't the same thing." Undaunted, Timothy continued, "You have a family to come home to after volunteering. Charlotte has her job and church, that's it." Timothy hoped to soften his wife's heart by the picture he was painting. Although Helen did feel for Charlotte's situation, she was not entirely convinced that Charlotte would wish it any other way. Maybe she had never dreamed of marriage and a family the way Helen had.

"I don't know who told her I needed the extra help," Helen remarked, trying to trace her way back to the issue at hand. "I know it must look like I need it, but the Christmas pageants are always rough early on. I never know how they are going to come together, but they always do. God has a way of working all the kinks out."

Timothy waited a moment before responding. The conversation he had initiated had lasted far beyond his expectations. He did not wish to mince words with his wife anymore, yet he felt the need to say one thing more.

"I know what you mean when you say that God has a way of working things out," he began, his tone gentle and subdued. "But, did you ever think that His way might involve Charlotte this time?"

Helen turned away from her husband, feeling the attacks had only followed her home from the church. She had thought that Timothy would see things her way; instead, he was trying to evaluate the situation from a higher perspective. Helen grimaced at the thought that the Lord would want her to spend the next two weeks trying to direct the play, manage the children, and get along with Charlotte all at the same time.

After the initial sting subsided, Helen's thoughts drifted slowly back to Charlotte. She would have come home this evening to only a feline audience of two. Is that why she had been so chatty at practice?

Helen could hear Timothy's words reverberate in her mind, "God's way might involve Charlotte this time." She could feel the conviction flood her soul as if the Holy Spirit were confirming the counsel she'd been given.

"I guess I never thought of it that way," she finally admitted, feeling half ashamed. Even though Timothy could not see the look on his wife's face, he recognized from her voice that her mood had softened. "You're probably right," she continued, "God would have me get along with Charlotte. I don't know how I'm going to do it, but I'll try to see it that way."

Now that Helen felt she had exhausted all verbal responses, she turned to look back at Timothy. She almost expected to glimpse a look of triumph, yet his features were soft and his brown eyes twinkling.

"That's what I love about you," he replied with admiration, before sealing his words with a kiss. Helen almost blushed at his words and gesture. How could she have been fuming with anger toward him just moments ago?

Reaching for Timothy's hand, Helen whispered, "I love you too."

Eleven

One More Obstacle

Although she had anticipated weeks of struggle, Helen found that she could do more than tolerate Charlotte's presence at the children's play practices. Once she became used to Charlotte's ways, Helen began to understand and appreciate her. It was easy to see that Charlotte truly desired to be a help. While it might be in her nature to take charge, she was more respectful of Helen's direction after the first night, and asked less questions. With the one exception, the children seemed to behave better after Charlotte's arrival. They were eager to please "Miss Sanders", and once Charlotte's objectives became aligned with Helen's, she served to channel their energies in the right direction. While Helen might have become jealous of the children's allegiance, she contented herself with the progress they were making. Maddy had found time to join others in working on the stage since Charlotte had taken over some of her responsibilities, and it seemed that, simultaneously, the program and set were coming together.

Just as a host of clouds fly away to reveal a vibrant sun, the days on Helen's calendar passed by until only one remained before the performance. While Helen was greatly pleased with the progress the children had made, she was still anxious about the final curtain call. While she reminded herself that it was a church program meant to glorify God, and that neither He nor the audience would be upset if the children made some mistakes here and there, her perfectionistic tendencies motivated her to do everything in her power to make sure the evening ran smoothly.

The day of dress rehearsal was a tiresome one for Helen. In addition to working her seasonal part-time job, she had to pick up the poinsettias to decorate the stage, create certificates of participation for each child, and comfort Krissie concerning her role in the play.

"Ith not fair," Krissie commented out-of-the-blue while Helen was hurriedly designing the certificates on her desktop computer. Helen had recognized something was on her daughter's mind a moment before when she had come into the living room without a word, her arms folded across her chest and her face forlorn. Taking her eyes off her work, Helen was relieved to find no trace of tears on Krissie's face. She hoped whatever the matter was it might be quickly resolved.

"What *is not fair*?" Helen asked, trying to enunciate every word properly for Krissie's sake. Krissie thought it really unkind that she should be reminded of her lisp at a time like this, but still in need of motherly comfort, she tried her best to speak slowly and clearly.

"Well," the little girl began, "it's just that Jenny gets to play Mary while all I get to do is be in the choir." Krissie let out a sigh as she sank into a large armchair that looked as though it would swallow her up in one gulp.

Helen was forced to curb her own frustration as she asked herself why Krissie had waited until the night of dress rehearsal to express her feelings. Perhaps it had only just occurred to her that Jenny would be performing before a large audience and not just Helen and Charlotte. Krissie had always been a little performer.

"Krissie," Helen said gently, pulling up a chair beside her daughter, "what would you say if we didn't have a choir in the Christmas program this year?" The concept was so foreign to Krissie's mind that she could hardly think of a reply.

"Well...I...but...we always have a choir."

"Just suppose we didn't," Helen continued, hoping that Krissie would follow her line of thought. Krissie wrinkled her freckled nose, a sign to those who knew her that she was in deep contemplation.

"I don't think it would be a very good program," she pronounced at last. Krissie had not been in more than a few pageants, yet each one had featured a choir. How strange it was for her mother to suggest a program without one!

"So, you think a choir is important?" Helen asked, pleased with the progress of their little talk so far.

"Well, yeah," Krissie responded without thinking. Slowly she began to understand what her mother was trying to say. The program needed a choir and she was part of one. It might be nice to play the role of Mary and hold the baby Jesus doll, but Jenny didn't get to sing. Krissie loved singing. The more she thought about it, the more she realized her part was not so bad after all.

Coming out of her reflections, Krissie was surprised to see her mother once again at the computer, typing as quickly as her fingers would allow.

"Mommy," Krissie began hesitantly, not convinced the conversation had truly ended, "aren't you going to ask me more questions?"

Glancing at her from across the room, Helen replied, "I don't think there's any need to."

Helen felt a chill rush through her as she reached to shut the van door. Alex and Krissie were already yards away from her, running around in the snow-covered field next to the church parking lot. Helen looked up just in time to see Alex throw a snowball at Krissie who immediately began to cry.

It's going to be a long night, Helen thought to herself as she rushed to take care of the situation.

Helen could hear the heat pipes rattling throughout the church building as she entered it, making the only noises other than her two children. A quick glance at her watch showed the time to be a quarter after six. *Charlotte had said she might be a little late*, Helen thought to herself. *I just hope she's here when practice starts at six-thirty.*

Since she had a few minutes of down time, Helen decided to fetch the children's costumes from the storage room. The mere thought of the costumes caused her to involuntarily sigh. The garments had been worn in every Christmas production since the time Maddy was in choir. Helen wished the church could afford to buy the children some new ones, but considered doing so would not be the greatest investment since the costumes were only worn on rare occasions.

Before heading to the storage room, Helen instructed Alex and Krissie to sit quietly until her return. They were not to run, jump, or yell. Given such instructions to follow, both were surprised a few moments later to hear Helen let out a wild scream that echoed throughout the empty building. Jumping out of their seats, Alex and Krissie ran to the storage room only to find their mother with her head in her hands, sobbing. A quick inspection of the room revealed the trouble right away. A puddle of water covered the tile floor, and more was still leaking out of a pipe that ran across the ceiling. Directly underneath the busted pipe hung all the costumes, drenched with water and dripping onto the already covered floor.

"Oh, Mom!" Alex burst out sympathetically. Feeling powerless and ashamed, Helen could not turn to face her children. She needed to be strong for them, but felt she had come to the end of her resources. Krissie's quiet sobs only added to her self-reproach.

"Are we going to have to cancel the play?" Krissie asked, tears streaming down her rosy cheeks. In an uncommon gesture, Alex moved nearer to his sister and put his arm around her shoulder. Before Helen could respond to her daughter's question, she heard someone behind her answer with a definitive, "no!" Turning around, Helen saw Charlotte as she knelt beside Krissie and held her close. Helen was not sure how long

Charlotte had been listening, but she guessed she had arrived in time to grasp the seriousness of the situation.

Although Krissie was soon comforted, Helen remained skeptical that everything would turn out right after all. They needed a plumber fast. Who knew how long the water had been leaking? The costumes might be ruined completely. There would be little time to find new ones, and even then, the church couldn't afford to buy them. The children had worked so hard; Helen could not disappoint them and their families.

The children. Quickly Helen glanced at her watch. Panic seized her as she realized the children would be arriving for dress rehearsal in less than fifteen minutes. What would she do? How could she possibly compose herself in such a short amount of time?

Charlotte's sharp movements brought Helen out of her reflections. The latter watched in amazement as Charlotte collected the costumes in plastic bags, placed buckets under the leaky pipe, and began to fill them with the water she was hurriedly mopping from the floor. Charlotte's calm and meditated actions appeared so natural it was as if she had performed the drill several times before.

"Okay," Charlotte said, pausing to catch her breath and consider the next course of action. Although Helen had been annoyed by Charlotte's confidence when the two first began working together, she was now ready to do whatever her friend commanded of her. Thankfully Charlotte did not keep her waiting long.

"The kids will start arriving soon," she began almost in a whisper. Taking a deep breath, she continued, "I'll take care of cleaning up this mess and getting in touch with a plumber. Meanwhile, why don't you go wait for the children? You might ask the parents if they would be willing to pick their children up half-an-hour earlier than we planned. Tell them we have a little situation, but it will be taken care of by tomorrow night."

Helen found herself feeling exceedingly grateful for Charlotte's wise direction. She shuddered to think what might have happened if she were left to handle the situation herself. Transfixed for a moment, Helen could hear the words she had heard just once before, “His way might involve Charlotte this time.”

Twelve

Behind the Scenes

In spite of herself, Helen continued to be anxious about the children's program. True, Charlotte had managed to track down a plumber. True, she had promised to find new costumes for the children. In a way, Helen felt half-ashamed of her lack of participation in the crisis. Charlotte had shouldered most of the burden herself, yet she had insisted on being allowed to find new costumes. Helen secretly wondered if the costumes she chose would really be suitable or whether Charlotte would follow her artistic fancies. *At least the children will have new costumes*, she had to remind herself throughout the day. *That is what I wanted after all.*

The Evergreens enjoyed an early dinner together before Helen, Maddy, Alex, and Krissie headed out into the brisk December night. Timothy and Kevin promised to follow a little while later, having volunteered to put dinner away and do the dishes.

Helen was amazed at how well the storage room looked as she inspected it. She was glad the plumber was not still in the building, otherwise she might have been inclined to hug him for the work he had done and how much it meant to her. Observing the empty rack where the dripping costumes had hung the night before, Helen's curiosity became almost as great as the children's to see what Charlotte had chosen.

Charlotte was late in arriving; by the time she entered the sanctuary the children were already lined up on stage and Helen was beginning to cue the prelude music. Even from a distance Helen could tell that Charlotte looked pale and careworn, and she began to blame herself for not insisting to help her. Charlotte enlisted Maddy's help to carry the costumes into the sanctuary. Then the two began handing them out to the children.

Helen inspected each costume and was more than pleased with Charlotte's choices. The costumes looked authentic, even from up close. She had never seen anything like them in the department stores. If she didn't know better, she would guess they were homemade.

“What do you think?” Charlotte asked hesitantly, after approaching Helen when her task was through. Her green eyes seemed to be searching for approval and Helen was quick to respond.

“I think they’re wonderful,” she answered with animation. “They look better than any I’ve ever seen in a store. In fact, they almost look as if you made them yourself.”

“I did,” Charlotte affirmed, catching her friend off guard. “I noticed when I began working with you how much the children needed new costumes. I decided to make them some myself since I enjoy sewing so much. I bought some patterns and even measured some of the kids when you weren’t around. I was afraid I might not have them done in time so I didn’t tell them what I had in mind.”

“I bet that was difficult with Krissie around,” Helen commented with a smile. “If she saw you measuring some of the others, I’m sure she would have become suspicious.”

Charlotte laughed, amazed at Helen's knowledge of her daughter. “It was a challenge, especially with Krissie,” she continued. “Yet, when I made it into a game, they all complied wonderfully.”

Still awestruck by the situation, Helen commented, “I didn’t even know that you could sew.” Although she tried to hide it, Charlotte's expression revealed disappointment, and

Helen quickly realized she had underestimated her friend's abilities. While the two had spent a number of hours together working with the children's program, there had been little time for personal chat.

"I'm sorry," was Helen's heartfelt response. "I can tell by your work that you've been sewing for some time."

"Almost twenty-five years."

"Then I imagine you didn't have too much trouble with these."

"Well," Charlotte answered, thinking over the last few weeks, "I did have one problem. I had to store the costumes where my cats couldn't get to them. Percy was very insulted that I shut him out of his favorite room."

"What's so funny?" one of the children on stage asked a moment later, wondering what good joke his directors were enjoying. It was enough to rouse the two women from their conversation, yet as Charlotte turned toward the children, Helen detained her.

"I can't tell you how thankful I am that you came to help me," she admitted, her eyes filling with tears. "Whoever told you I needed help knew what they were talking about."

Remembering the night she had come to offer her services, Charlotte shook her head in contradiction. "No one told me you needed help," she replied simply. "I just felt like I should volunteer. I guess the Lord was really working behind the scenes of this production."

Thirteen

Charlotte's Confession

Christmas had come and gone faster than anyone would have believed possible. The time had been precious, but much too short to suit Molly's tastes. She had been delayed one day of travel due to a heavy blanketing of snow that had fallen across much of the Midwest. When at last she arrived at her parent's home, she spent much time catching up with the rest of the family and enjoying the traditions she had known since childhood.

Yet, while she was glad to be "back home" for a few days, Molly missed her new home, not the empty apartment she had left, but the warm and loving place she remembered it to be before Jared went away. She had always looked forward to creating her own holiday traditions with her husband someday. *Someday* still seemed so far away.

On a chilly New Year's Eve afternoon, Maddy was curled up on the sofa with a book, while her siblings enjoyed the fresh snowfall, and Helen busied herself making snacks for the evening festivities. Alex and Krissie were more excited than any of the others that day, since only on New Year's Eve were they allowed to stay up past midnight if they behaved.

Helen had just pulled a tray of cookies out of the oven when the phone rang. Maddy answered it and Helen could hear her talking from the other room.

"Oh, hi Charlotte," she was saying. "Yeah, Mom's here. Hold on just a sec." Maddy came into the kitchen with the cordless phone in her hand. Helen brushed her hands on her apron, then took the phone from Maddy. *I wonder what Charlotte wants to talk about*, she thought to herself.

After their initial greetings, Charlotte informed Helen of the reason for her call. "I know it's short notice, but I really need someone to talk to. I was wondering if you would be willing to have coffee with me at the little café in town. I understand if you can't make it."

Although Helen had planned on icing the cookies after they cooled, she told Charlotte she would meet her at the café in twenty minutes. Charging Maddy to make sure the others did not stay outside too long, Helen put on her winter apparel and headed out the door. The quiet moments she spent driving gave her mind time to wander. What was it that Charlotte wanted to talk about? Had something happened to someone in her family? Why had she sounded so serious? Of all the people Charlotte could have called to talk to, why had she chosen her?

Meeting up with Charlotte at the café, Helen quickly recognized the impression of tears on her face. Charlotte's ordinarily cheerful green eyes appeared glazed and swollen. Her hair was pulled up in a careless knot behind her head, and her vibrant smile was replaced by a dull grin.

"I'm glad you could make it," Charlotte admitted, after she and Helen had located a table for two hidden in the back corner at a distance from other customers. Even the choice of seating warned Helen that the issue weighing on Charlotte's mind was not a minor one.

"I don't know what I would have done if I'd had to stay inside today," Charlotte continued. "Even Blanche was afraid of me. She's been hiding under the bed all day." Charlotte attempted to laugh, but Helen could see that it took concentrated effort. Without knowing what plagued her friend, Helen wondered if it would even be in her power to be an encouragement to her. She just prayed she wouldn't offer any unfeeling advice. Hearing Charlotte mention one of her cats, Helen thought that might be a safe subject to introduce again into their conversation.

"Blanche is a pretty name for a cat," she commented. "I imagine she's all white."

"Yes, except for a few specks of orange around her ears," Charlotte replied easily enough. "When she stands next to Percy they look like good versus evil. Percy is all black. I can't spot him in the dark. I've stepped on him on several occasions."

Charlotte's words trailed off as the waitress came to take their orders. Charlotte and Helen spent the next few minutes chatting on various topics, with neither one revealing much more than she might tell a stranger. However, almost as soon as the waitress had left after bringing their coffee, Charlotte spoke up again. The tone of her voice and her countenance were entirely altered.

"Well, I'm sure you can guess I didn't ask you here to talk about my cats," she began. Helen studied Charlotte's face as she spoke. Her eyes looked soft and vulnerable, while her pursed lips told of her determination to reveal what was on her mind. Helen's slight nod gave her permission to continue.

"Well, the reason I wanted to get out and talk to you today is because New Year's has bad associations for me. I can never forget what happened this night many years ago." As Charlotte paused for a breath, Helen considered the limited information with which she had been entrusted. Helen knew little of Charlotte's family, but she was aware her father had passed away at a young age. Perhaps it had happened on New Year's Eve. *How horrible that would have been!* Helen thought to herself.

Helen's mind was so focused on other possibilities that she was completely unprepared for what Charlotte told her next. "I know you don't know, nobody around here does, but I was engaged once." In just a few brief words, Charlotte completely shattered Helen's picture of her. While Helen knew that Charlotte loved children, she had supposed she was content as a single individual. She never seemed to regret her situation in life, yet at one time she had been headed in a different direction. *What had prevented the marriage?* Helen's mind could hardly slow down enough for her to hear Charlotte as she continued.

"We were going to be married on Valentine's Day. I remember I was so excited that it happened to fall on a Saturday that year. Anyway, most of the plans had already been made for the wedding. Then, on New Year's Day, around one in the morning..." Charlotte choked on her words. Her face suddenly became flushed and she almost despaired of finishing. Tears had begun to well up in her eyes, but she quickly brushed them aside.

Without knowing the circumstances, Helen felt compassion rising in her soul for the woman beside her, who had been carrying a heavy burden for many years, unknown to much of the world around her. Whatever had happened to Charlotte that day had changed her considerably, and left her with scars that remained even now.

Setting her jaw, Charlotte picked up where she had left off, "Around one in the morning, Peter was driving me home from a New Year's Eve party. The roads were really bad that night. Peter had not had anything to drink and he was driving sensibly. The driver who hit us was drunk. He ran the red light and crashed into the driver's side of Peter's car."

Charlotte was aware that her hands were shaking, but she could not still them. The events that had taken place over fifteen years ago were still so vivid in her mind it seemed as if she were experiencing them all over again. She began to wish she had not told Helen of her grief and disappointment. How could Helen, the happy wife and mother of five children, possibly sympathize with her situation? For a moment Charlotte despised Helen as the representation of all that she had lost that dreadful night. Then, remembering how she had once found peace within the loving arms of her Heavenly Father, Charlotte rebuked herself. Helen had no more ability to arrange the details of her life than she had. The Lord had written both their stories; it had been His will to take Peter that night, even though Charlotte would never understand why. Her fiancé had loved the Lord and filled his days ministering to the poor and giving generously of his time and resources to further the kingdom of God. The answer to why his life had been snuffed out in the chill of that winter night belonged to Someone greater than herself.

Looking up into the eyes of the friend she had envied just moments before, Charlotte glimpsed the genuine compassion gleaming through the tear-stained face. Knowing now that she was not speaking to an unfeeling acquaintance, but a sympathetic friend, who possessed the ability to comfort another by her quiet, understanding presence, rather than by her empty words, Charlotte found the strength to finish her narrative.

"Peter was killed instantly. Even though a bystander who had witnessed the accident called for help immediately, it was no use. He was gone and I was left with a pain that plagued me more on the inside than any I was experiencing on the outside." Having related the most painful details of the story, Charlotte breathed a sigh of relief. She reached for her cup to take another sip of coffee, then studied Helen as she searched for something to say in response.

"I'm so sorry; I never knew," was all she could manage.

"I didn't expect you to," Charlotte answered honestly. "I haven't told anyone since I moved here."

"Did you move here to...get away from it all?" Helen's voice betrayed her hesitation; she hoped she was not probing too far into her friend's affairs by her question. After hearing about her past, Helen no longer wondered about certain facets of Charlotte's personality. She imagined her sometimes overbearing confidence was meant to conceal the hurt and disappointment she had experienced. Charlotte was generally so cheerful; she had not allowed the circumstances of life to dictate her outlook. Helen's respect for Charlotte soared as she considered how she had found comfort in the Lord instead of turning against Him and living a life of bitterness. Remembering all that she had said of Charlotte that first night after her appearance at practice, Helen lowered her gaze in disgrace, only to look up again when Charlotte carefully answered her question.

"Yes, I moved to Missouri as a way of escaping, I guess," she admitted. "I had grown up in a small town in Illinois where everyone seemed to know everyone. After Peter died, I didn't feel I could look people in the face anymore. I had everyone's sympathy, love, and even anger directed at the drunk driver, but I couldn't stay.

"I found a position teaching here and I left behind all I had known to start a new life. I never told anyone what had happened to me, although a number of people were puzzled at why I didn't seem to want to get married. I was twenty-five and had attracted the gaze of several nice young men, but I didn't want to marry just for the sake of being married. No one could replace what I had lost." Charlotte was breathing a little freer now, as Helen gently asked her why she had chosen her as a confidante.

"It was time, past time, to let it go," Charlotte responded. "I've tried not to be bitter or blame God for what happened, but I think I've kept this secret for too long. It was beginning to wear on me. I knew I could trust you not to gossip about me. Plus, you were the only one home."

Charlotte laughed freely, but Helen struggled to hide her annoyance that she had been chosen merely as a last resort. Then she remembered how little she had done in the past to show herself worthy of Charlotte's confidence. Charlotte had been more honest in her answer than Helen had been in evaluating herself as a friend.

Afraid that Charlotte planned to spend the evening alone with her disturbing memories rather than with friends issuing in the New Year, Helen made an invitation.

"My family is heading over the Phillips' home tonight to celebrate. I'm sure Suzie wouldn't mind if you joined us and I'll ask her if you want." Smiling, Helen added, "That is, if you don't mind being around a bunch of rambunctious kids!"

"Are you kidding?" Charlotte asked incredulously.

A few moments passed easily before Helen broke the silence. "Are you still close to your family?" she inquired gently, before finishing her last sip of coffee.

"Oh, yes," Charlotte answered, her eyes lighting up. "We don't see each other too often, but we keep in touch by phone and e-mail a lot. My dad passed away a number of years ago, but I still go to see my mom and two brothers and their families when I can. I never go over the holidays though. Mom asks me every year, but I can never seem to bring myself to go." Helen nodded her head understandingly, as Charlotte reached for her purse and stood up from the table. Helen buttoned up her heavy coat and tucked a bright purple scarf, compliments of Krissie, about her neck.

"Thanks again," Charlotte told Helen as the two parted ways en route to their cars.

"Don't mention it," Helen replied candidly, remembering all that Charlotte had done for her in helping with the play. "I'll see you tonight," she added as she waved goodbye.

Fourteen

Invitations

The New Year brought with it new hopes and dreams for the Evergreen family, as each member held a special wish in his or her heart for the year to come. Even if nothing happened beyond the expected, it would surely be an era of change. A new life would introduce Molly to motherhood, while turning her younger brothers and sisters into uncles and aunts, and Timothy and Helen into grandparents. Maddy would graduate from high school, to her great dismay, while to his great joy, Kevin would test for his driver's license. While a few upcoming events held more excitement for some than others, there was one dream that was near to everyone's heart. Although Molly wished it most of all, her family joined her in hoping and praying that Jared might soon come home.

For Krissie, one of the greatest events of the New Year was the celebration of her birthday. Born the last day of January, Krissie's focus for almost the entire month was on her party. She wanted to invite far more people than her small home could accommodate. Although Helen gave Krissie the liberty of making a list, she warned her in advance that she would be helping her weed through it before they sent the invitations.

The number of guests Krissie had dreamed up was no surprise to Helen, however, she was taken aback at the sight of Wesley's name on her long list. It had never occurred to her that Krissie might want to invite her former pal to her party since

Helen had come to accept Wesley's indefinite absence from their family's future festivities. Unable to explain her reasoning, Helen had a difficult time convincing Krissie that Wesley could not be invited. Krissie knew nothing beyond what was visible of the situation between her sister and Wesley. She knew Wesley never came to her house anymore, never called Maddy anymore, and never sat beside them at church as he used to do. In all her childish naiveté, Krissie could not understand what had initiated such an unfavorable turn of events.

"I miss Wesley, Mom," Krissie admitted to her mother as the two were narrowing down her choices. "I want him to come."

"I know you do," Helen responded carefully, "but just because you want Wesley to come, doesn't mean that he should." Krissie wrinkled her blond eyebrows as she pondered her mother's statement. *Why shouldn't Wesley come?* she asked herself. He wasn't mad at her and she was sure she hadn't done anything to make him upset. Helen sometimes told Krissie that she used "poor logic" in her appeals for something she wanted badly enough to use any excuse she could dream up to win her mother over. To Krissie, Helen's reasoning for not inviting Wesley to her party was "poor logic".

"But why shouldn't he?" Krissie asked, becoming sulky and sticking out her bottom lip. "He always told me I was like the little sister he never had. I know he would come if I asked him."

"Which you won't," Helen interjected, her expression so resolved it allowed Krissie no room for argument.

Lowering her head, she responded, "Okay, I guess you can cross him off my list."

Although Wesley Underwood's name had scarcely been mentioned in the Evergreen household for months, one exception being Krissie's failed attempt to invite him to her birthday party, it just so happened that the Sunday following Krissie's conversation with her mother, Wesley broke the silence between himself and the family. Krissie had seen Wesley at church that day, but she had expected him to only smile and walk past her as he had done many times before. To her great surprise and delight, however, he stopped to wish her a happy birthday.

"Now," he said in a mock-serious tone while bending down next to her in the foyer, "if I'm not mistaken, someone I know is going to be having a birthday real soon." A wide smile spread across Krissie's face as Wesley spoke to her. Even though they had not spoken in some time, Wesley had not forgotten her birthday. How thoughtful he was!

"You remembered!" Krissie exclaimed, her eyes twinkling in the winter sunlight that was shining through the panes of glass in the foyer.

"Of course I remembered," Wesley answered, pleased to see that Krissie held no grudge against him for the long void in his communication with her. Speaking like his old self again, he added, "How could I forget my little sister's birthday?" His words thrilled Krissie, who reached to give him a hug. Becoming a little self-conscious of the spectacle he was creating, Wesley broke free from her embrace and stood up, smoothing the fresh wrinkles on his dress shirt. Krissie was too deep in thought to notice or take offense at Wesley's action. Although Wesley could tell Krissie's mind was preoccupied with something, he had not the slightest idea of what it might be. He thought that mentioning her birthday again might cheer her up, but he soon realized that her birthday was the very thing that was troubling her.

"Are you having a birthday party?" he asked, raising his eyebrows and trying to appear excited for her sake. As he spoke, Krissie's countenance fell. Why did he have to mention her party? Here he had been so good to wish her a happy birthday, and she was not allowed to invite him to her party. She began feeling guilty and she worried that he would never forgive her for not inviting him to a party in which he had taken interest.

"Yes," she answered honestly with a sigh, "I'm having a party."

"Is it all that bad?" Wesley inquired, clearly perplexed at the girl's lack of enthusiasm. Krissie's eyes were fixed on the floor; she could not look at Wesley. She was afraid to see his reaction when she would be forced to tell him that he could not come to her party.

"Don't you want to have a party?" Wesley probed further, before Krissie told him all.

"It's not the party, really," Krissie answered, as tears began gathering in her eyes. "It's just that Mommy told me I couldn't invite you to my party. I think she thinks you wouldn't want to come."

Finally understanding Krissie's burden, Wesley put a brotherly hand on her shoulder. He was not always the best at knowing what to say in situations like these, but he tried to choose his words carefully.

"Your mommy is very smart, you know," he began, knowing full well the reason behind Helen's decree. "She only wants everyone to be comfortable and have a good time at your party."

"But wouldn't you have a good time, Wesley?" Krissie asked innocently. The anxious look in her eyes made Wesley uncomfortable. He shifted his weight from one foot to the other and looked distractedly at the people around them. It was true that he loved Krissie and her family and would enjoy celebrating with them on this occasion. It was his feelings for one member of her family in particular, however, that made him uneasy about responding.

It was when he could no longer bear the intensity of Krissie's gaze as her sad eyes stared into his that Wesley spoke. The words had scarcely left his mouth when he began to regret them.

"Tell you what," he had said, "if no one else in your family objects, I'd be willing to come to your party."

"Oh!" Krissie exclaimed, clapping her hands together excitedly, "I'm so glad! I'm sure no one will mind."

Remembering the clause he had included in his offer, Wesley emphasized it again. "Be sure to ask them *all* if it's okay," he reminded her. "After all, I can cause a lot of trouble at birthday parties. You know, one time I blew out someone else's candles." Wesley laughed, but Krissie did not see the humor in his confession. She could not picture an adult, such as Wesley, blowing out a child's candles. Wesley had not told her that he was just five years old when he had performed the shameful act that had caused his young cousin to cry for a good half-hour. Blowing out another's candles was no laughing matter, Krissie reflected. Why, it was almost criminal!

Shaking Wesley's comment about the candles from her mind, Krissie promised to ask her family if he could come to her party. "I'll tell you for sure next week," she said. "I know they won't mind." As Krissie walked away, Wesley contemplated the conversation he had just had.

Amazed at his own forthrightness, he thought to himself, "I can't believe I just invited myself to an eight-year-old's birthday party!"

That afternoon while her family was eating lunch, Krissie revealed the news she had been anxiously keeping inside.

"Guess who I talked to today at church?" she asked, full of anticipation. When no one immediately ventured a guess, Maddy took advantage of the opportunity to tease her little sister.

"Anthony, maybe?" Maddy suggested. Krissie blushed at the mention of the preacher's son who was two years her senior and who she had admired for the last year or so.

"No, Wesley," she replied matter-of-factly, allowing the red on her cheeks to quickly alternate between tints of embarrassment and anger. Suddenly Maddy became the one who looked uncomfortable and whose cheeks were flushed. Unable to ask any of the myriad of questions that came to her mind, Maddy had to depend on her mother's ability to get to the heart of the issue, which she did without delay.

"You talked to Wesley?" Helen asked her youngest daughter in confirmation.

"Yes," Krissie responded from across the table, "and guess what he said?" She paused a moment, but filled in the missing information herself when no one offered any suggestions. "He told me if none of us said 'no' he would come to my party!"

"All right!" Alex exclaimed with more emotion than he was accustomed to show. "I can't wait to see him again! I bet he could show me how to finish my model airplane." Alex concluded his last sentence with a glare at his brother seated next to him. Kevin had tried unsuccessfully on two separate occasions to put the final pieces of the airplane together. Clearly the younger boy was frustrated with his brother's failed attempts and was ready to let someone else try his hand at the project. His words were a challenge to Kevin, who had realized years before that he was not as handy as he might like to be.

Interjecting with frustration apparent in her voice, Helen asked, "Has it occurred to any of you that I just might have had a reason for not allowing Krissie to invite Wesley? There are..." Before she could continue speaking, Maddy stopped her.

"Mom, I don't mind Wesley coming if it's all right with you." Maddy had been thinking since Krissie's last speech that if Wesley had consented to come, he must be getting over his disappointment over last year's homecoming. If he did not mind seeing her, she would not mind seeing him. In fact, being together again might provide some much needed closure worth the few hours of awkwardness.

Feeling that she was grossly outnumbered, Helen told a jubilant Krissie that Wesley might come to her party. At the same time she said that she wanted to know all the particulars of Krissie's discussion with him. Although Krissie felt that some sort of punishment was eminent, she still rejoiced at the happy prospect before her.

Fifteen

Long-time Friends

After the main events of Krissie's birthday party were over, her guests stood chatting merrily amongst themselves. Everyone seemed to be in good humor, except for Maddy and Wesley, who had barely spoken to one another during the course of the afternoon. Although both desired to initiate some sort of conversation, various distractions and fears had kept them from getting anywhere with their plans. They had bumped into each other only once, for which they both apologized. While the majority of guests were clueless as to the tensions that existed in their midst, Krissie could not fail to notice how Maddy and Wesley were behaving and she felt it her duty to try to make peace between them. Breaking from the game she'd been playing with her cousin, Krissie approached Wesley just as he was helping himself to a second piece of cake. It just so happened that Maddy was within earshot at the particular moment, and what she overheard both startled and mortified her.

"Don't you like my sister anymore?" Krissie asked bluntly, almost causing Wesley to drop his cake on the floor. Although he instinctively looked up to see if Maddy were around, Wesley needn't have bothered. Just a moment after the words had left Krissie's lips, Maddy had stepped up behind her sister and whispered her sharp rebuke. Wesley could feel the increased tempo of his heart as he recognized the difficult explanation before him, but he tried his best to appear composed.

He smiled, sat his cake down on the table beside him, and bent down on his knees in order to give Krissie his full attention. He did not make any attempt to lower his voice, and Maddy knew that he was speaking for an audience of two, not one.

"Of course I still like your sister," Wesley began, his words sounding as easy and sincere as he could make them. While Krissie naturally trusted Wesley to tell the truth, his confession did not lessen her confusion.

"Then why don't you talk to her anymore?" she implored. Wesley took a moment in responding, shifting uncomfortably in his crouched position. He wanted to phrase his words carefully and to avoid both lying and revealing too much. To Maddy, his momentary pause seemed to last much longer.

"Krissie," Wesley said, drawing the little girl into his conversation.

"Yes?"

"Do you know how long Maddy and I have been friends?" When Krissie did not answer in words and shrugged her shoulders, Wesley told her. "We've been friends since before you were born. Every friendship has its ups and downs. Just because Maddy and I aren't as friendly to each other as we used to be doesn't mean we're not still friends." Krissie looked back at her sister and then focused her gaze once again upon Wesley. She seemed satisfied, and although Wesley had fulfilled his obligation to Krissie, he wanted to make the most of the opportunity.

"Maddy and I have been friends for ten years," he summarized. In a lower tone he added, "And I hope we always will be."

Wesley patted a smiling Krissie on the shoulder and then stood to return to his cake. Helen called for Maddy's assistance from another room and Maddy dutifully went to help her mother. She had hardly time to let Wesley's words sink in, yet she felt as if a ray of hope had found its way to her troubled soul.

A half-hour later, Krissie's party came to a close. Krissie said goodbye to each guest, while bravely fighting back tears. She especially hated to see her cousin, Tessa, go. Although they lived several hours apart, the two girls were great friends and always seemed to pick up right where they had left off.

Maddy hoped she would have a chance to speak with Wesley before he left. She was glad that no one was around as he was heading to his car. She ran out the front door and yelled his name, causing him to stop in his place. Wesley felt awkward enough given the situation, and hesitated to trace his way back to Maddy, so he was relieved when she made the effort to catch up with him.

"I'm glad I caught you before you left," Maddy said breathlessly. Wesley offered nothing in response; he merely forced a smile, hoping to appear less uncomfortable than he really was.

"I wanted to ask you something," Maddy explained. She was beginning to feel uncomfortable herself and wanted to get straight to the point. "Did you mean what you said in there, or was that just for Krissie?"

Wesley looked at Maddy for a moment. He could not help wishing she cared for him the way he cared for her. To him, she would always be beautiful. Even now he was distracted watching the strands of her auburn hair escape from their up-do and blow about her face. Yet, his attraction to Maddy went much deeper than physical appearance. He might find another beauty, but he despaired of ever finding someone whose company he would always welcome or whose presence would comfort him the way Maddy's did. He told himself that some things just were not meant to be, but it did not take away his remorse.

Glancing down quickly in order to regain his composure, Wesley admitted, "I couldn't lie to you or to Krissie. I can't help the way I feel, Maddy, but I don't want to lose you completely. I hope that in time..." Wesley did not finish his thought, but he did not need to. Maddy understood completely what he was saying, and she hoped that, given time, she and Wesley could be friends again. Still, Maddy knew things could never be the way they had been. They were not children anymore with childish problems that could be easily remedied. Life was more complicated now, and solutions to its problems were less complete than they used to be.

Maddy watched as Wesley's car backed out of her driveway and into the street. The sun was just setting, and its vibrant orange color was only enhanced by the pale pink and purple streamers surrounding it in the winter sky. Maddy returned Wesley's wave as he drove away, before reaching down to rub her shoulder. The wind was picking up outside and she quickly realized she had forgotten her jacket. Even though the weather was mild for late January, it was much too cold for her short-sleeve dress.

As she began to head inside, Maddy's mind turned to the night of homecoming. She remembered feeling at that time like the whole world was crashing down on her. Now, things were different. Now, it seemed as if she and Wesley might renew their friendship. Even if that never came to pass, Maddy still looked forward to a brighter future than she could have at all anticipated just months before. Since homecoming, Maddy had learned more clearly where her hope should lie and felt more prepared for other challenges that might come her way.

Sixteen

Beginning Again

"Is this it?" Tristan Parker asked his father, Nick, as the latter pulled their car into the driveway of a seasoned ranch home. The dull, gray color of the stone, and the window shutters faded from their original blue to closely resemble the shade of the brick, seemed to match the enthusiasm Tristan felt for his family's new living arrangements. Still, in spite of his dissatisfaction, the boy tried to appear pleased. He was at an age where he had come to realize that the feelings he expressed had an effect on those around him, and he felt it his duty to be as positive as possible around his father, who was already carrying a heavy load.

"This is it," Nick answered in a subdued tone, as he turned off the car engine. After a full day of travel, during which he had found himself trying to entertain his boys in the back seat and mediate their disputes while managing to drive safely, Nick was exhausted. His body yearned for rest, yet he knew no sleep could subdue the pain that plagued his heart day and night. He sought in vain to repress the memories, and it only increased the somberness of his mood and frustrated his concentration on other things. He knew that he had made a decision that would affect him and his boys for years to come. He only hoped he had made the right one.

In spite of the host of other thoughts that were running through his mind, Nick turned his attention to Tristan, and his younger brother, Nolan, who sat still staring out the window as if his family had yet many hours left to drive. Recognizing the stale quality of his answer to Tristan's question, Nick addressed a challenge to his older son, who seemed at least aware of his surroundings and ready for instruction.

"I wonder who can get all of their things unloaded first," he remarked with forced excitement. Tristan responded immediately by removing his seatbelt and trying to bolt out of the car.

"Dad!" he exclaimed in frustration after failing to escape. "I can't get out unless you unlock the doors!"

"Oh, right," Nick apologized, amused enough at his son's sincerity to allow himself a slight laugh. He quickly remedied his mistake by clicking the power door lock button by his side. Nick was glad that Tristan seemed so ready to spring into action; he only wished that another could say something to him that would motivate him so readily. He sympathized with Nolan and felt no more ready than the young boy to embark on this new journey, let alone to lead the way.

"Come on, Nolan!" Tristan urged his brother after he had climbed out of the vehicle. Although he wanted to come forth as the victor of the race, it would mean nothing if his opponent did not at least attempt to participate. Nolan had not even unbuckled his seatbelt and he seemed to have no immediate desire to get out of the car, though his family had been driving for nearly seven hours that day.

"What's the matter, son?" Nolan's father asked him. Still sitting in the front seat of the vehicle, Nick monitored the boy by adjusting the rear view mirror to where he could view the back seat behind him.

"Is this our new home?" Nolan asked disappointedly. Before Nick could respond, Tristan chimed in.

"Of course it is," he answered confidently, and quite unlike someone who had just a moment before become privileged to the information. "I just asked Dad that."

Trying to draw Nolan into the conversation once again, Nick asked in reference to their new house, "What do you think?" This time Nick turned around in his seat in anticipation of his son's answer. He raised his dark eyebrows interestedly and softened his look as if to assure Nolan that he could speak freely.

Inspecting the building in front of him, Nolan replied with the blunt honesty of a four-year-old, "It's ugly." While Tristan immediately began to rebuke his brother, Nick stopped him. Even though he had only had seven years of experience as a father, Nick had learned children do not always speak with the most easily discernible motives at heart. To be sure, the structure in front of them was far from impressive. The mounting gray clouds telling of a winter snow shower only helped to enhance the drab exterior of the building. Very little about the scene in front of them seemed to testify to life. The house seemed to be in mourning in much the same way they were. While the homes on either side of it were colorfully decorated with brightly shaded hunter green and burgundy shutters and vibrant red brick, this house had been left behind. It existed in the midst of vitality and color, yet it appeared lifeless and dull. Still, Nick couldn't help but wonder if what Nolan found so disgusting about the home really had nothing at all to do with its appearance. Perhaps any home would seem just as repulsive to him, since each would lack his loving mother's presence. With such a prospect to consider, Nick could not blame Nolan for finding the house ugly. After all, he felt the same way.

For days Nicholas Parker questioned whether or not he had done the right thing in taking his boys from the home they had known all their lives. To be sure, when he heard of the job opening, Nick jumped at the chance to leave the place that held only painful memories for him anymore. He loved new adventures and would have moved several times before had not Karen kept him anchored in Indiana. While this move was hardly his idea of an adventure, he felt it was necessary for his own well-being. Still, he hated to watch Tristan and Nolan adjust to a new environment after they had already lost so much.

Nick's own loss was always before him. There was a vacancy in every corner of the home, surpassed only by the one in his heart. He had managed somehow to endure the funeral and the compassion of family and friends. He was reminded time and again by his mother that "God had a reason" and that he would only find solace if he surrendered his burden to the Lord, yet how could he go to the One who had taken his wife away from him?

Nick's life for many years was largely characterized by blessings, the result, he supposed, of his decision to trust the Lord with his life. Yet, his commitment had never been challenged in a serious way before. Karen's illness had been so sudden; he had only months to prepare himself for her death. He had pleaded with God that he could not do without her, but apparently his prayers had gone unheeded.

While Nick might not have admitted it to himself, he knew that he was purposely neglecting finding a new church in Missouri. Although his life was full of new and time-consuming challenges, he had time enough to feel the weight of the conviction. Somewhere between settling into a new job and home and caring for his boys, Nick realized he was leaving the most important things undone. He was successful at brushing the feeling aside for the first few weeks, until he had an unexpected confrontation with his son.

Thinking his boys were safely tucked away in bed, Nick took advantage of the solitude to flip through a family photo album. Within a few moments, his eyes were too full to see the pictures. Casting the album aside, he stretched his lean frame across his mattress and buried his face in a pillow. Lost in his grief, Nick failed to hear a slight rapping at his door.

"Dad?" a small voice called, followed by another knock.

Now aware of his visitor, Nick hollered back, "Just a minute." The delay was hardly adequate for him to regain his composure, but it gave him just enough time to dry his face and conceal the album under a pillow.

"Come in," he said at last. Quietly the brass door knob turned and Tristan appeared from behind the door. Nick studied his son's face in hopes of discovering any information about what was on the boy's mind before he volunteered it. He came to no conclusion, however, as Tristan's countenance held no signs of tears or pain. He only looked serious and perhaps a little scared in the watchful eyes of his father.

"What's wrong? Why aren't you asleep?" Nick asked gruffly. He was merely trying to compensate for his recent lapse into tears, but he could tell from Tristan's expression that he had tried too hard.

"I couldn't sleep," the boy responded, fearing he should have chosen another time to ask his father something. Nick noticed the anxiety in Tristan's voice and tried to make himself more approachable. Inviting his son to sit beside him on the bed, Nick assured Tristan that he would do his best to help him overcome whatever was causing his insomnia. Secretly Nick hoped it had nothing to do with Karen. How could he comfort his son over the loss of his mother when he was still grieving for her? When Nick learned of Tristan's concerns he was both relieved and surprised.

"I wanted to ask you something," Tristan explained, after Nick inquired more gently a second time about what was troubling him. "Why don't we go to church anymore?"

Tristan's words gave Nick the sensation of having a bucket of cold water poured over his head. He had excused his conduct to himself, but how could he explain it to his son?

"I don't know," he replied automatically, before sinking lower in his own eyes. *First I make excuses, then I lie to my son? What have I become?* he asked himself.

"No, I *do* know," Nick corrected a moment later. Tristan's eyes grew as he saw the discomfort apparent in his father's features and waited for his explanation.

“I've been hiding, Tris. Hiding from God.” The words came freely, but unexpectedly. Nick was stunned by his own honesty and immediately began to wonder whether or not he had been right in sharing his struggle with his son. What kind of example was he setting after all? Could Tristan possibly understand what he meant?

“Oh, you mean like Jonah?” came the innocent reply. Nick smiled and laid his hand on his son's shoulder.

“Yes, like Jonah. He ran away from God when he was told to go to Nineveh.” It was easy for Nick to re-tell the story he knew so well, yet he stumbled over the words for his own. “I ran away from God when...He...took your mommy away.”

“But He took her to heaven,” Tristan added, looking full into his father's face with an earnest look of comfort mixed with confusion.

“Yes, He did.” Nick fought every moment to hold back tears. He had thought so much in recent months of what he had lost. Tristan's words reminded him of what he still possessed.

“Tell you what,” he began, “I'll spend some time this week scouting around and, on Sunday, I'll take both you and Nolan to church. Is it a deal?”

Tristan smiled and agreed to the proposal. He left his father's room with a much lighter heart than when he entered it.

After tucking Tristan back in bed, Nick returned to his room and found the photo album still hidden in its place beneath a pillow. As his eyes scanned the photographs once again, Nick's heartache was replaced by remorse. Seeing Karen's bright smile in nearly every picture taken of her, Nick realized he had failed his wife in the course of just a few short months. Nothing would have kept Karen from taking the boys to church.

Suddenly realizing there was One he had wronged worse than Karen, Nick fell to his knees against the side of his bed. For a long time he remained, praying for forgiveness and guidance. When at last Nick fell into bed, he succumbed to a more restful sleep than he had known since Karen's death.

Seventeen

Visitors

It's just going to be one of those days, Charlotte thought to herself the Sunday morning following her scheduled visit with family. Although she had planned to return home Saturday in time to get a decent amount of rest before teaching Sunday school, an over-turned semi-truck had put her behind schedule. When at last she crawled into bed it was already the wee hours of Sunday morning.

Charlotte had enjoyed her three-day visit to Illinois. "Back home" she was a much beloved daughter, sister, and aunt. While her trip was technically a vacation, it had been exhausting. Charlotte never slept well away from her home, even when she was "back home". She missed her cats, and sinking into that comfortable spot in her mattress that, after years of service, had come to outline her figure perfectly.

All things considered, it was no wonder that Charlotte overslept on her first night back. When she woke up Sunday morning she instantly began making preparations for the day; yet, for all her effort, she was still a good ten minutes behind schedule.

Arriving at the church, Charlotte became thankful for the first time that most of her children generally appeared late. She hoped she could manage to walk into her classroom without a soul knowing she was running behind. However, as she neared the doorway, her hopes were dashed as she spied a man and his son waiting silently for her arrival.

Of all the days for me to be late, Charlotte reproached herself, *it had to be the day we have visitors!*

Overcoming her embarrassment, Charlotte smiled and introduced herself to the man, who until a moment before had been sitting in one of the children's small plastic chairs. Upon seeing her enter, he stood up and smoothed the front of his shirt and pants.

"I'm Nick Parker," the man replied coolly. "This is my son, Nolan," he added, gesturing to the small blond-haired boy beside him.

"How are you, Nolan?" Charlotte asked. He did not answer, but hid behind his father instead. Charlotte did not press him further; she knew it took some children longer than others to warm up to adults other than their parents.

"I'm sorry I was late," Charlotte admitted rather awkwardly. "It doesn't usually happen. It's just that I got home late last night from seeing my family." Charlotte tried to make eye contact with the man, but he seemed to be studying everything around the room other than her. She almost wondered if he had even heard her speak, but his abrupt reply answered her thoughts.

"Oh, that's all right." The words were polite, but the man's eyes still avoided contact with those of his listener. "Nolan and I only arrived here a few minutes ago along with Tristan, Nolan's older brother. This is our first Sunday visiting and I was told by one of the greeter's that you were a fine teacher and would be sure to be here." As Nick spoke, he tried to lure Nolan out from hiding behind him. The little boy shook his head, however, and refused to move an inch forward.

Trying to make conversation, Charlotte commented on the boys' names. She told Nick that she thought they were both excellent choices.

"Yeah...well, their..." Nick began to say, before a lump formed in his throat. Unable to speak further, he was relieved when another child entered the classroom with her parents.

"Miss Sanders!" the little girl exclaimed, while running up to her teacher to give her a hug.

"How are you, Katie?" Charlotte asked fondly, grateful for a distraction from her perplexing conversation with Mr. Parker. Katie's loyalty breathed into Charlotte the confidence she needed after her discouraging start to the day.

"I'm fine," Katie grinned, lost in her teacher's attention. Seeing their daughter happily engaged, Katie's parents quietly slipped away.

While Charlotte and Katie were chatting about the dress the little girl was wearing and various other things, Nick continued to try to make Nolan more at ease about attending the Sunday school class.

"I'll only be gone for one hour," Nick assured his son. He had already knelt down to be closer to Nolan's eye level; now he rested his hand on the boy's head. "Can you be good for Miss Charlotte during that hour?" he asked coaxingly.

Hearing her name, Charlotte's eyes quickly traced the route from Katie to the father and son several feet away from her. She smiled as warmly as she knew how at Nolan, but he only nodded in agreement to his father's question. Nick was satisfied. If Nolan had made any arguments, he would have been afraid to leave him in the class. As it was, he seemed willing to at least tolerate the situation. From what Nick had seen of Katie's interaction with her teacher, Charlotte was a capable individual. Nick always felt that children could be fairly decent judges of character.

Even though the situation was momentarily under control, Nick felt the need to establish a Plan B just in case. It occurred to him how hard any separation must be for Nolan after losing his mother so suddenly.

“I’ll be in the adult classroom upstairs,” Nick told Charlotte, while looking across the room at Nolan. “Please don’t hesitate to find me if you have any problems.”

Charlotte could not help wondering why Nick had not looked her in the eyes for more than a few seconds at a time during his conversation with her. Although he was communicative, he seemed no less shy than his young son, who had just now gone to play by himself in the corner.

“I don’t think we’ll have any problems,” Charlotte replied optimistically, while flipping through her children’s Bible as one last reminder of the day’s lesson. She did not like looking at a man who would not return the favor. Yet, as she thanked Nick for the concern he had shown in making his whereabouts known, her eyes instinctively trailed upward. To her surprise, Mr. Parker was looking back at her with an expression just as mysterious as his previous failure to make eye contact.

Eighteen

A New Arrival

It was a little after noon when Charlotte arrived home from church. The day was still young, and yet from the time she entered the door until she fell asleep that night, Charlotte could not shake the image of Nick Parker from her mind. She kept pondering her brief interactions with him and her experiences with Nolan. It didn't take much observation to perceive the two were both suffering in some way. While Nolan might be naturally shy, Charlotte was convinced from his polite, but somber behavior that he was unhappy. He'd chosen to play by himself when he had the liberty, but was quick to join the others for the lesson when Charlotte told him to. Without knowing his circumstances, Charlotte felt her heart warming toward her little pupil. She hoped in time she could win his trust.

If Nolan was a mystery to Charlotte, his father was more so. It was common for children to be afraid of new people and surroundings, but Charlotte had never seen an adult look so uncomfortable, especially when it was clear he had given careful thought to his appearance. Nick's long-sleeve shirt and pants had been pressed so as to remove even the hint of wrinkles, and they seemed a perfect match for his tall, lean frame. Charlotte had no scruple admitting that her visitor was a fine looking man. While she noticed some gray intermixed with his wavy black hair, it seemed only to make him look more sophisticated. A few wrinkles stood beneath his light brown eyes, eyes that appeared to hold volumes but reveal very little.

Throughout her solitary lunch, Charlotte reconsidered all she had learned of the Parkers. Nick had spoken of Nolan's brother, Tristan, but had not mentioned one word about his wife. Perhaps Mrs. Parker was not a Christian. Charlotte hated to consider the possibility that Nick was divorced, but imagined it would account for the sadness she had seen in the man and his son. The only other alternative she could dream up was that Nick's wife had passed away.

What am I doing? Charlotte asked herself a moment later. *I know how much it bothered me when people speculated about my past when I moved here. Now I've been doing the same thing!*

Although Charlotte determined not to invent any more histories for the Parker family, she could not help thinking of them as the week progressed. As she finalized her lesson plan on Saturday a disturbing revelation came to her. What if Mr. Parker and his son were not at church the following day? What if her rare tardiness had upset Nick more than he allowed? Charlotte began to feel foolish for thinking so much about people she might never see again. Yet, she was genuinely concerned for them. Whatever their history, they clearly needed comfort and support. Charlotte prayed that, whether it was in her congregation or another, they would find what they needed, and soon.

As Molly flipped her calendar, a bit of red ink immediately caught her eye. Months ago she had circled her due date, imaging at the time how slowly the days before it would pass. Although she had been counting the weeks anxiously, the little red circle still took her by surprise. As she stared at it, her mind was drawn in another direction. It had been the better part of a year since Jared left home, and there was no hope of him returning before his first child was born. Molly had arranged for her mother to come and stay with her around the time of her due date and had other plans in case the baby came sooner. Every time Molly spoke to Jared on the phone or received an e-mail from him, she could read his disappointment at not being home to care for her. His words were cheerful enough, but she knew he felt the same way she did.

Before two weeks had passed, Molly found herself nervously awaiting her mother's arrival. Her contractions had begun in the early morning hours. Helen had called from the airport twenty minutes ago. *She should be here any minute,* Molly reassured herself.

Molly started as she heard the chimes reverberate throughout the bottom floor of the apartment. She went to the door as quickly as she could, but to her dismay, it was not her mother who was standing at her doorstep.

Heather blinked at the sight of her friend, pale and grimacing with pain. She led Molly back to the couch as quickly as she could, then asked for directions.

"Are you okay? Do you want me to take you to the hospital? When did it start?" she blurted out almost in one breath.

"I'm fine. My contractions are still far apart," Molly replied coolly, trying to force a smile. "Mom should be here any minute."

Heather tried to believe her friend and follow her instructions, but it was all she could do not to rush Molly to the hospital that very moment. She didn't have to struggle long, however, as an SUV pulled up in front of the house the very moment Heather had finished hauling all of Molly's prepared luggage to the door.

"I'm so glad to see you!" Heather said abruptly, opening the apartment door wide. Helen was startled, to say the least.

"I'm sorry, do I know you?" she responded carefully. "I thought this was my daughter's apartment, but perhaps I have the wrong place."

"No, no, no" Heather answered quickly. "This is the right place. Molly's here waiting for you. She needs to be taken to the hospital."

Now Helen moved with unprecedented speed. Within minutes she and Heather had loaded everything into the vehicle and were en route to the hospital. While Helen had never met Heather before, she already felt she owed her an enormous debt of gratitude for helping her daughter, and now acting as a reliable navigator since Helen was unfamiliar with the area.

The Lord timed this one perfectly, Helen thought to herself, *although, I wouldn't have minded a less eventful welcome!*

A little less than six hours later, Molly was resting contently on her hospital bed, holding a sleeping baby boy by her side. Helen was sitting in a rocking chair beside her. While her body followed the chair's movements, her eyes were locked on her new grandson. Although she hadn't needed anyone else to affirm the truth, Helen had been pleased when the doctor and nurses described Molly's child as "beautiful". He had some wisps of blond hair on his round head, which could only be seen upon careful inspection. His eyes, on the other hand, needed no special examination. They stood out beneath his light eyelashes like two blue-green pools. To the great amazement of many, they seemed to follow much of what was going on close to them.

Each time Molly looked upon her son's face, she saw the face of another who had the exact same shade of eyes. Although her heart was soaring beyond anything she had ever before experienced, it still ached at the thought of her husband far away, unable to witness his son's birth. While Molly and Jared had previously agreed on a name, Molly still felt as if she were stealing a pleasure from Jared when she gave instructions for the baby's birth certificate to read, "Ethan Michael Weaver".

Late that night in the hospital room, Helen called her husband and told him to turn the phone on speakerphone and gather all their children around it. When she was assured everyone was present, Helen handed the hospital phone to Molly, who, for a moment, was unable to think of a way to pass along her happy news.

At last she said, "Hey, do you all feel any different? You have a new nephew today! Ethan Michael is right here beside me." Molly choked as she added, "He wishes you all could be here to see him."

Suddenly a chorus of excited voices rang over the phone line. It was so loud, Molly temporarily pulled the receiver away from her ear. Still, she managed to hear her brothers and sisters claiming their new titles of uncles and aunts. Molly wished she could see their faces. She almost laughed at the thought of Krissie, now a most unlikely aunt. No doubt she was already proud of herself.

At last the other voices quieted and Timothy switched the connection to the receiver so that he could speak directly to his daughter. He struggled to find words to say. His daughter and son-in-law had made him so happy. Even though he had not witnessed the birth, he could imagine Molly lying in her hospital bed, glowing with a new mother's radiance. He wondered what his little grandson looked like and which parent he more closely resembled. He was so thankful that the day was indeed a day of joy, with no anxieties for the health of either mother or child. While Timothy had been unable to keep a watchful eye over his daughter, her Heavenly Father had taken very good care of her. Tears welled up in Timothy's eyes as he asked Molly how she was doing and brokenly tried to tell her how much he loved her. Even in the midst of the excitement and overwhelming joy that Molly felt, she could not keep herself from crying. She heard the emotion in her father's voice as much as she might have seen it in his eyes had he been standing in her hospital room alongside her mother. Molly felt at that moment how blessed she was to have such loving parents. She saw for a few brief moments how connected her mother's life was to her own and how, if it had not been for a similar event taking place over twenty-two years ago, neither she, nor her newborn son, would be present on this happy day.

The conversation between father and daughter did not last long, since neither one was composed enough to say much in words. Yet, for years to come both Timothy and Molly counted it as a precious memory not to be forgotten.

Molly e-mailed Jared as soon as she was able, sending along a few photos of their new son. Jared's reply was brief, but it made Molly both laugh and cry almost simultaneously. She printed a copy of it and put in in her journal. For weeks to come whenever she looked at Ethan, she remembered his father's words, “I hope you don't mind me saying so, but he seems to look a lot like me.” *No, I don't mind*, Molly said to herself, *I don't mind one bit.*

Nineteen

Revelations

While Charlotte had wondered if she'd thought too much of the Parker family when it was uncertain that she would ever see them again, she had no real reason for alarm. For almost eight weeks straight, Nicholas Parker brought his two boys to Sunday school and church, the one exception being the week Nolan was sick. Although Charlotte still found Mr. Parker to be reserved and non-conversational, Nolan began to warm up to her after spending a few weeks in her classroom. He began volunteering to pass out papers or snacks or put the chairs under the table. He tried to help when he thought the other children were not watching, lest they think he was vying for special attention. It was still a struggle for Nolan to answer questions or recite Bible memory verses, but Charlotte's gentle eyes gave him the courage he needed. Charlotte could not help but fall in love with her little pupil as she witnessed his eagerness to please. She wished she knew more of his background and what it was that still troubled him. When she asked him, Nolan always replied that he enjoyed the preschool he was attending. What was his home life like?

One afternoon when Helen stopped by Charlotte's house to use her superior sewing machine for a project, she asked Charlotte how her current Sunday school class was progressing. Charlotte remarked that it was going well and that she had two new students, one of whom was Nolan Parker.

"I've made Nolan my special project this year. He captured my heart from the very beginning when he could do little more than remain quiet and try to tolerate his time in my class. Now he really enjoys it. He doesn't always show it, but I can tell he looks forward to coming." Shaking her head she added, "He seems too old for his four years."

Helen nodded her head, a look of understanding on her face. Suddenly Charlotte's ears were wide open. Her eyes asked the question that her mouth would not and Helen read their meaning.

"I take it you don't know about Nolan's family," Helen began hesitantly. Charlotte gently shook her head. Taking a deep breath, Helen considered whether or not she should continue. Mr. Parker had labored to tell her and her husband the truth several weeks ago. Perhaps it would be better for him to be spared repeating the story to every person he met. In any case, the truth would come out sometime. "The Parkers didn't start coming to our church immediately, but they haven't been in the area long. You see, Nick's wife passed away last year and it's been very difficult for him."

As Helen finished, Charlotte felt her heart drop within her. *Mr. Parker was a widower?* She struggled to believe it. His wife would have been so young. *What had happened?*

As if Helen had overheard her friend's last question, she continued to explain. "Apparently, Mrs. Parker, Karen was her name, contracted a fast-spreading form of cancer. They didn't discover it in time for treatment to be of much use. Nick was devastated. If you haven't noticed, he seems almost cold initially. When he first came over for lunch, he was very polite, but didn't seem ready to tell us about himself. We talked about his boys and his job and things like that, but he said little that was personal. It wasn't until last month that we learned this much of his history."

"I'm stunned," Charlotte replied honestly. Of course, Helen couldn't have known how much the Parkers had been on her mind in recent weeks.

"Timothy and I are so glad he and his boys are coming to church now," Helen commented, changing the path of the discussion. "He admitted to us one afternoon that he had quit attending church and that it was Tristan who helped convince him to come back."

"Poor child," Charlotte whispered, her eyes moist with tears. The more she considered the Parker family's situation, the more she felt for them. Tristan and Nolan had lost their mother before they'd begun to encounter the greatest obstacles that life was sure to bring their way.

"Which stitch should I use for this?" Helen asked abruptly, bringing Charlotte back to the topic of sewing. Within half-an-hour, Helen's project was complete and she was hugging Charlotte and thanking her for her help.

You helped me too, Charlotte thought to herself.

Although Charlotte had been surprised to learn of Nick Parker's tragic loss from her friend, as it happened, she would not have had to wait long to hear it from the man himself. The truth was, Nick was more than pleased at how Nolan had warmed to Charlotte. He seemed to anticipate Sunday more than any other day of the week. *Quite a change since our arrival here,* Nick admitted to himself. *Seems like he didn't even smile before.*

After the morning service was over, Nick instructed Tristan and Nolan to wait for him and went in search of Charlotte. He wanted to thank her for all she had done for his son, even if it meant revealing more than was comfortable.

"You certainly have a way with Nolan," Nick began. "He's always talking about you. Even when we go shopping he thinks about you. He sees random items and says you would like them. It took me fifteen minutes one time to persuade him that you didn't want a certain picture album."

Charlotte's face lit up at the story. She almost remarked teasingly that he might have been wrong about the picture album, and inadvertently lied to his son. However, before Charlotte had the chance to say anything, Nick's tone became more serious.

"I don't know if you've heard it from someone else, but my wife passed away last year. It's been really difficult for me and the boys. I doubted a number of times that I was doing the right thing in moving out here. I wasn't exactly listening to the Lord's voice as I should have been at the time, but I know He's forgiven me now. Anyway, I see a number of evidences that I made the right move, whether my motives were right or not. You're one of those clues, I think. Nolan has opened up so much since I first brought him here a few months ago." Nick paused for a few moments to consider what he meant to say. Meanwhile, Charlotte's heart began beating faster as her mind explored the possible paths this conversation might take.

"I wondered..." Nick said at length, "I wondered if you wouldn't be interested in babysitting my boys on occasion. I've been invited by some of the men in my office to go golfing, but I can hardly take the boys with me. I didn't really have much of a heart to get out initially, but I think it might be good for me now. We'd go out on a Saturday so it shouldn't interfere with your work or anything. If you're not interested, that's fine. I've thought of asking Mrs. Evergreen, but I think she's got her hands full already. You don't have to let me know today." Nick added this last statement as an aside since Charlotte had failed to give any indications of her thoughts. In truth, she had been surprised by the whole conversation, and her reaction to it. Nick had never been talkative, especially when it came to personal matters. *What was I thinking? He just admitted he hasn't had the heart to go golfing and I think he might be pursuing another relationship?*

"I'd love to watch the boys," Charlotte responded finally. "I don't know Tristan other than by sight, but I'd enjoy getting to know him. Is he as much of a character as Nolan can be when he tries?"

"Worse," Nick replied honestly. "I think Nolan is trying to match Tristan's sense of humor as well as his height."

Charlotte smiled, but her mind was a jumble of questions.

Twenty

Perspectives

As Nick headed toward home, he asked his boys about the time they had spent with Charlotte that afternoon. Apparently Tristan had made friends with both of Charlotte's cats. His exposure to the friendly felines had left him wondering if he could persuade his dad to get him a pet. He brought the question up somewhat casually, but Nick caught his meaning and assured him that it was not the right time to bring a cat into the family. Tristan heaved a little sigh of resignation, but was soon engaged again in telling his father about his afternoon.

"Miss Sanders let me and Nolan help her fix some cookies. They turned out really good," he commented with satisfaction.

"I guess I'll be able to judge that when I get home," Nick replied smiling. "Charlotte sent a few home with me."

"She's really nice," Nolan chimed in for the first time. He was always ready to stand up for his teacher, even when, as in the present situation, it was hardly necessary.

"Dad?" The high tone of Tristan's voice gave warning that something was weighing on his mind. "How come Miss Sanders doesn't have any kids?" Nick choked at the frankness of his son's question. How could he answer honestly, but carefully? It wasn't that Tristan hadn't sprung similar questions on him before. At least he had waited to ask this one in private. From his naive perspective, Charlotte was a very nice woman who was good around children. Yes, she was alone, but then, their father was now alone as well. Somehow it didn't seem right to Tristan that Charlotte should be by herself when she had apparently enjoyed their company so much.

Swallowing hard and giving himself a minute to comprise an answer, Nick began, "Well, Charlotte's not married. She doesn't have a family."

"She doesn't have a mommy and daddy?" Nolan asked confused. Nick wished he didn't have to drive while answering his boys probing questions. Some minor road construction ahead slowed him down and caused him to focus more on his driving. He was thankful for the intermission it gave him.

"No, Charlotte has a mommy and a daddy, but she isn't a mommy. Do you understand?" Nick asked his younger son, who already had been told something of the sort by his older brother, but who only now took it as absolute truth since it had come from his father. Now that Nolan's curiosity was satisfied, Tristan began to ask more questions.

"But why isn't Charlotte married?" In his own little world, Tristan found that most things in life made sense, except for the loss of his mother. Why was it that everything could be mixed up in the adult realm?

"I don't know," Nick answered honestly. The thought had crossed his mind a number of times in recent months. He too saw that Charlotte seemed well suited for the family life, but lived alone. He would not try to understand why; he only knew that he appreciated her willingness to work with his boys inside and outside of her Sunday school classroom. She was filling a need they had that he could not fill. He would always be grateful for her presence in their lives during such a difficult time.

Once at home, Tristan and Nolan became caught up in play, leaving Nick to recover from his stressful commute. Yet the boys' questions remained with him throughout the evening. He wished he knew more of Charlotte Sanders.

Molly watched from outside the door as Maddy adjusted her cap in the bathroom mirror. *Strange how fast time passes,* she thought.

Maddy did not know her sister was nearby until she saw her reflection in the mirror. Startled, her body flinched as she let out a small shriek.

"Shh..." Molly quickly charged, holding her forefinger to her lips like an elementary school teacher. "Ethan is sleeping in the other room." Molly was not very serious about protecting her son from excess noise, as few things generally disturbed his rest. She merely wanted to take the opportunity to tease her little sister. Such windows were small since Molly lived a distance away.

"I can't help screaming if you sneak up on me," Maddy quickly asserted in her own defense. She held her serious posture for a moment before breaking into laughter. Even though much had changed since Molly left home, it was a comfort and a pleasure to Maddy to interact with her sister as she did in years past. Especially today, which marked a turning point in her life, and one for which she was not wholly prepared.

"I can't believe my little sister is graduating today," Molly commented a little condescendingly.

"Hey, it was bound to happen sometime," Maddy replied, her tone a little heavier than it had been as the anxieties she had came back into focus.

"Are you sorry it's happening now?" Molly seemed to read her sister's thoughts. Maddy nodded her head affirmatively and, as she did, her eyes began to fill with tears that she at once tried to shake away.

"Hey," Molly said, her facial expression urging her sister not to put on an act in front of her. "I know what you must be feeling. Change is difficult and uncertainty is worse, but you'll get through."

Maddy's eyes rose to meet her sister's. For a moment she questioned what right Molly had to tell her this. Then the truth struck her like a forceful gale. Molly, if anyone, knew the meaning of change. She had been a wife with a husband at home, then not long after, a husband overseas. She had become a mother miles from those about whom she most cared, excepting her mother. She had dealt daily with the realities of Jared's situation, his safety, his absence. Nearly everyone graduated, but few experienced all the struggles that Molly had had in such a short period of time. At that moment, Maddy began to admire her sister more than ever before. She reached out to hug her and whispered in her ear, "I miss you, you know". Both were crying now, aware of the changing circumstances of life, but holding fast to the promise of God's unchanging love.

As he passed by the bathroom, Timothy found his two eldest daughters wiping away their tears. They were a little more at ease now and were talking about the various details of Maddy's graduation party that their family was hosting that evening. *Their laughter hasn't changed*, Timothy thought to himself as he stopped to listen to them. He could hardly believe it was already time for his second child to be graduating from high school. He and Helen had spoken much about this in private. Although both were more prepared to see Maddy graduate than they had been with Molly, it was still a struggle. Helen found some comfort in the fact that Maddy would not be moving out any time soon. They couldn't afford to send her away to college and Maddy preferred to remain at home anyway. Although Helen knew that Maddy would be easier once she had settled on a path, she was almost as anxious as Maddy to see where that path might lead.

"Are you ready to go?" Timothy asked his daughters, finally interrupting their conversation.

"As ready as I'll ever be," Maddy replied honestly.

Twenty-One

News

It was a drizzly autumn afternoon and Ethan was sleeping soundly in his crib. Although Molly had struggled for half-an-hour to induce him to fall asleep, she felt that the credit for his slumber was due more to the steady rainfall outside than to her own efforts. Taking advantage of the precious quiet time, Molly curled up with a blanket and a novel she'd been waiting some time to read. Not more than twenty minutes had elapsed before her solitude was interrupted by the telephone's sudden tone. Molly jumped out of her chair in a mad dash to answer the call before Ethan started stirring.

She had little time to guess who her caller might be. She didn't recognize the voice that responded to her greeting, and was almost prepared to end the conversation, assuming it had been initiated merely for sales purposes. Then a sudden thought hit her.

"Mrs. Weaver?" a gentleman's rough voice came over the line. Although many might address her in this fashion, Molly intuitively felt she now knew the purpose of this call.

"Yes, this is she," she answered meekly, her eyes already filling with tears. Although she dreaded the next words that would reach her ears, she still wished they would come sooner rather than later. Each moment brought images to her mind of Jared in danger, missing in action, or worse. When at last she learned the truth of his whereabouts and situation, she was already in hysterics and momentarily unable to find any hope in the news she received.

"I'm sorry to have to tell you this, ma'am, but your husband's been injured." The gentleman paused a moment, leaving Molly's mind a whirlwind of questions. Thankfully many were answered in the caller's next breath, even though it seemed ages to Molly before the silence was broken.

"He sustained a blow to the shoulder," the deep, steady voice continued, "but is expected to make a full recovery. He's being brought back to the States for medical treatment." In a slightly softer tone came the words, "I'm sorry." Molly could sense the compassion of this man she had never met. As she struggled to make sense of everything she'd just heard, the conversation fell silent.

"Are you all right, Mrs. Weaver?" the man asked, fearing Molly had not been strong enough for the news. She could not answer; her mind was full only of Jared.

"I'm all right, or I will be," Molly spoke at length. "Thank you for letting me know."

After putting the phone back on its base, Molly stood momentarily numb. Just a few short minutes had changed so much. For the first time since the news broke, she began to feel relieved. Jared was injured, but he would recover. And he was coming back to the States! Soon she would be able to sleep at night knowing he was no longer surrounded by war. *He'll be coming home!*

In spite of these thoughts, Molly soon found herself in a flood of tears as she considered all that Jared had been through during his tour of duty. True, life had been difficult for her, but Jared had suffered the most. Soon they would be reunited and, hopefully, be able to put some things behind them. Molly prayed that Jared would readjust quickly to the life he had known.

Molly was so absorbed in her thoughts that it took a few moments before her mind was clear enough to respond to her now wide awake son. Ethan was crying, a little louder every minute.

Lifting him into her arms and wiping away the large tears that had begun to run down his face without first stopping to dry her own, Molly began to pour forth words of comfort and affirmation that worked to quiet him in a just a few minutes' time. Little did she think as she was consoling Ethan that she was ministering to her own heart as well. Even though the words had become unnecessary as Ethan was now calm and had begun to drift off to sleep, she continued to repeat, "You're fine. It's okay. Everything is going to be all right."

Twenty-Two

Romantic Interests

Nick heard the clock chime one in the morning as he continued to pace silently across the floor. He could not sleep no matter how he tried. Too many thoughts were awake in his mind for his body to be asleep. Each one centered on certain feelings that failed to go away. The more he tried to tell himself not to care for Charlotte, the more he seemed to do so.

What kind of man am I? he asked himself. *Karen's been gone little more than a year and I'm already thinking of another relationship?*

Nick knew that both of his boys had become very attached to Charlotte. She seemed to fill a need they both had, but would she consider taking on a more permanent role in their lives?

As much as he tried to manipulate his feelings, Nick knew that his attraction to Charlotte was not merely founded in the belief that she would make a good mother for his boys. For all her own merits, Nick cared for her. She was a lively, cheerful spirit. Being around her made Nick feel he was constantly standing in sunshine. Her servant heart was evident from the way she handled the children both inside and outside her classroom. And then, although her youth had passed her by, she was beautiful, with her flowing red hair and sparkling eyes.

Turning around to sit on the edge of his bed, Nick sighed. There was only one thing to do.

Charlotte was engaged in the end of the novel when she heard the phone ring. She almost resolved not to answer it, wanting nothing to distract her from the stirring conclusion. Yet, knowing her mother had been scheduled for some minor hand surgery that day, and thinking the call might be an update on her condition, Charlotte reluctantly put down her book. Instantly she recognized that the caller was not either of her brothers. The man's tone was too deep and formal. Although he identified himself as Nick Parker, it took Charlotte a moment to grasp this. Nick had called her before when she was babysitting his boys to let her know if he would be late in arriving. Maybe he was calling to see if she was available to babysit this evening. If so, her book would have to lie idle for more than just a few minutes. Charlotte had a few eccentricities, one of which was being able to finish the end of a book or a movie in one sitting. Still, life was not about doing all the things she wanted to on her own time.

"I know this is going to come as a shock," Nick started hesitantly after a prolonged pause, immediately capturing Charlotte's attention. "I'm still shocked about it all myself."

Nick's words startled Charlotte. She almost feared something had happened to the boys, but Nick sounded too composed for that to be the case. Whatever the man was trying to say, it was apparently difficult for him.

"Yes?" Charlotte gently answered. She was trying to listen patiently, but the long silence only increased her anxiety.

"I don't know any other way to say it, Charlotte. You've been such a blessing to my boys. You've been such a blessing *to me.*" Another short pause elapsed. Charlotte numbly twisted the phone cord she held in her hand. She considered where this conversation might be headed, but that possibility was far too incredible.

"I've really enjoyed the time we've had together." Charlotte almost thought she heard Nick swallow a lump in his throat before continuing. "In fact, I've come to care for you as something more than just my boys' babysitter. If there's any way..."

"Mr. Parker," Charlotte interrupted, her words just above a whisper. It all seemed like a strange dream. Charlotte couldn't believe Nick had come to care for her, and so soon after his wife's death! She had to put a stop to this. Things were fine the way they were. She was glad to be a help to Tristan and Nolan. Maybe she'd been a little too friendly to Nick. Still, once he saw things correctly, everything could return to normal.

"I'm sorry," The words surprised Charlotte even as she said them. Was she really sorry she couldn't return his feelings? Or was it that she wouldn't even try? "I've enjoyed the time I've spent with you and your boys, but I don't want things to change. I'm happy as I am." *Am I even being honest?* Charlotte questioned herself.

After an awkward silence, Nick thanked Charlotte for her time and said goodbye. As Charlotte hung up the phone and returned to her cozy spot on the couch, she was immersed in a wave of emotions. She should feel relieved; after all, she had given Nick the answer to his question. Now she wouldn't have to worry when she saw him at church or when he dropped the boys off. *If he ever lets me babysit them again!* Charlotte thought, feeling her heart sink within her. Only now did Charlotte realize how much the two youngsters had added to her life. She believed she meant something to them as well. How would they feel if their father found another babysitter for them? Had her selfishness hurt more than Nick?

Picking up the novel that had her mesmerized just minutes before, Charlotte fanned the pages and idly attempted to pick up where she had left off. "It's no use," she said out loud and tossed it aside.

Pacing across her living room, Charlotte considered why she had been so quick to shut the door that Nick had opened between them. She felt sure of his sincerity and it only added to her guilty feelings. There was nothing inappropriate about their relationship taking on a different meaning. True, she was several years older than him, but if he didn't mind, why should she? Charlotte had always loved children. During the years she had struggled to keep her heart from becoming entangled in another relationship, Charlotte had been forced to realize she would never be the mother she had hoped to be. She thought of herself at times as a mother to the children in her Sunday school class, but it was by no means the same.

As these thoughts raced through her mind, Charlotte recognized that she was looking at her life like an outsider might. People were not game pieces to be placed wherever desirable openings arose. Life was so complicated. It wasn't that Charlotte merely loved children, but she had come to love Tristan and Nolan. How did she feel about their father? Hadn't she always enjoyed his company and looked forward to him picking the boys up from her home, not because she wished for them to leave, but because she wished to talk to him about how his day had gone?

All at once, images of another face flooded Charlotte's memory and she came to lose all doubts about her decision. She could still remember the day that Peter proposed, the happiest day of her life. She remembered looking into his eyes and pledging to herself that she would never find comfort in another. Peter's memory had sustained her for the past sixteen years. He had been the one for her. There was nothing else to consider.

Twenty-Three

A Change of Heart

On Sunday morning, Charlotte waited anxiously in her classroom for Nick to arrive with Nolan. Since her conversation with him three days ago, she had been dreading and anticipating this occasion. She hoped Nick had come to accept her answer. She wanted to see him smile again and talk with her in the old, carefree way.

Almost before she could understand the meaning behind it, Tristan came into Charlotte's classroom with his younger brother.

"Where's your father?" Charlotte addressed the older boy.

"Waiting down the hallway," Tristan replied honestly with a shrug. "He said he'd take me to class once I dropped Nolan off. I don't know what's going on." Tristan spoke with confusion apparent in his voice. He couldn't imagine why his dad didn't want to see Charlotte. There seemed to be no other explanation, since Nick was comparatively doing nothing waiting in the hall. What had happened? Tristan struggled to accept that the two people about whom he cared most seemed no longer on friendly terms.

Charlotte swallowed slowly, recognizing more fully how her conversation with Nick had impacted their relationship. Still, she hoped that this was only a temporary arrangement and that, once Nick had more time to think it through, he would come into her classroom again. Yet as the weeks passed, and the same scene was acted out again and again, Charlotte was forced to acknowledge that Nick had been affected more deeply than she had hoped. He hadn't called her to watch his boys since the time of their conversation. Although Nick may not have needed a babysitter during this time, Charlotte was more inclined to believe that he had found someone to replace her.

Beyond feeling remorse for how she had hurt Nick, Charlotte began to feel sorry for herself and the opportunity she had so carelessly tossed aside. She tried to reason these feelings away, but they kept coming back, each time with fuller conviction. Remembering her former conversations with Helen, Charlotte decided to seek counsel from one who knew more of Nick's history and her own than most others.

Helen was not aware of a double motive when Charlotte asked if she had time to "help shop for some items". Glad for an opportunity to spend some time away from home, Helen came along willingly. It was only after Charlotte had failed to make any selections during the first hour of their outing that Helen became suspicious.

"Is something on your mind?" Helen finally put words to her looks which had asked the same thing, but Charlotte seemed to ignore. Although she had desired Helen's advice, Charlotte now began to regret that she had taken this last step. She would have to admit what she had said to Nick, how she was feeling, and the irreconcilable ideals she continued to possess. She had not told anyone else about these things and no one would know unless she or Nick brought them up. Still, Charlotte knew she couldn't pretend like nothing had happened. That would be more miserable than any explanation or apology would be.

Finally resolved on her course, Charlotte told Helen all that had happened with Nick. Helen took it all in silently as a courtesy to Charlotte; however, she didn't feel she could have been forced to speak immediately had it been required. She was so amazed at Nick's change of heart. When her family had first known him, he had acted as if his life were over. Timothy had agreed with her that he was then the most downhearted individual he'd ever met. Yet, in the course of the same year, Nick had begun to pursue another relationship! Helen was encouraged to hear that he had come this far, yet she sympathized with him in Charlotte's refusal. Why had Charlotte turned him down?

"Can I ask, Charlotte, what made you say no?" Helen found courage to say. No doubt Charlotte had expected her friend to ask her this question; still, she struggled to answer it.

"Well, ever since Peter died, I guess I've believed that I wouldn't ever find anyone else. I've always thought that there is just one right person for everyone. I felt sure Peter was right for me and I made sure not to let anyone else replace him in my heart. Even though it's been a long time, I still can't forget him."

"No one is asking you to do that," Helen replied gently, while resting her hand on Charlotte's shoulder. The two had been looking at living room curtains, yet now everything around them seemed to fade out of existence. Charlotte eyes began to fill with tears, but she quickly checked them. Although she felt that happiness and fulfillment might be hers for the taking, she could not seem to advance a single step. How could she begin dating Nick and not feel that she had somehow forgotten her previous love?

"I remember when you told me your story," Helen commented, seeing that Charlotte had no immediate desire to say anything. "I was so surprised to hear about the details of your life. I never would have known that you had suffered so badly unless you had told me." Hitting upon a new idea, Helen continued. "Do you know why I wouldn't have known?" she asked. Charlotte merely rocked her head from side to side. "Because you moved on with life. You didn't think it was harmful to Peter's memory to keep working or living or shopping. Why is it so harmful to consider a new relationship?"

Charlotte sniffled as she looked up into her friend's eyes. Helen certainly did not possess the ability to reconcile all of her difficulties, but her view point was unique to any that Charlotte had considered before. Continuing with life had been a given; she hadn't questioned it. Yet, as Helen said, that too could have been seen as an insult to Peter had she taken her logic to the extreme. Was it truly this issue which now kept her from Nick, or was it the fear of being hurt in the same way twice? Charlotte wondered how she could expect others to probe her own heart when even she had not been able to discern its hidden motives.

Although Charlotte left the mall with her hands empty that day, her heart was full of promise as she determined to listen to its voice. There was one question, however, that nagged Charlotte constantly. *How can I explain myself to a man who won't even speak to me?* She wondered.

Twenty-Four

The Messenger

Charlotte had come no closer to an answer the following day, which was a Sunday and the only day she saw any members of the Parker family. Although she hoped that Nick might come into her classroom now that she was ready to see him in a different light, Tristan appeared as usual. *He doesn't know my feelings have changed,* Charlotte scolded herself. *He's still hurt. I can't blame him for not wanting to see me.*

As she wrapped up her Sunday school class and helped her pupils prepare to meet their parents, Charlotte's mind hit upon an idea. She rejected it instantly; surely no self-respecting adult would stoop *that* low. Yet, the hope the plan held outweighed the reservations Charlotte had. If only it could work as she envisioned it! She had exactly seven days to figure out what she wished to say. Would it be that easy?

"Come on, Nolan," Tristan urged his younger brother after Sunday school the following week. "Dad's waiting for us." Tristan had now become used to his role as Nolan's escort. He was starting to enjoy the responsibility it gave him. He liked being able to boss his younger brother around some.

"I'm coming," Nolan replied, grabbing his papers off the round, children's table. As he stopped to wish his teacher goodbye, she detained him.

"Remember what I said," Charlotte whispered, while trying not to make Tristan too suspicious. "Make sure no one sees it but him."

"What was that all about?" Tristan asked Nolan in the hallway. He knew that Charlotte had shared some secret with Nolan, but he didn't know anything about it. Nolan, however, was perfectly prepared to keep his mission a secret. He liked knowing something his older brother didn't know.

As the boys met their father in the hallway, Nick bent down to ask Nolan how his class had gone. Nolan told his father about the lesson he had learned and showed him the craft he made. He held out his hand of papers and Nick took a look at them. The first one was a sheet of once blank paper now covered by images recognizable only to their artist. The second was a scene from the Bible story that Nolan had decorated with stickers. The third was...a handwritten note? Nick looked again at the paper his son had been holding. What was he doing with a note from his teacher? Was this Charlotte's way of addressing a behavioral problem Nolan had? Why hadn't she just approached him about it?

As Nick inspected the paper further, he realized it had nothing at all to do with Nolan. Charlotte had apparently utilized one of her only opportunities of contacting him.

Dear Nick,

I wanted to apologize for how I handled our phone conversation several weeks ago. I didn't truly mean some of the things that I said and I've been looking for a way to tell you so. I hope you don't mind that I enlisted Nolan to help me out. I didn't know what else to do. I'm sorry that I've made things so difficult for everyone, but I really have had a change of heart. I hope you can forgive me and that we can work things out.

Sincerely,

Charlotte Sanders

Nick was stunned by both the message and its means of delivery. Had he made himself so unapproachable? Nick wanted to charge into Charlotte's classroom that very moment and admit his own guilt, but he was detained by the church bell that told of the fast-approaching service hour. A discussion would have to wait.

Charlotte had wondered many times if she had misused her position as a teacher to get Nick's attention, yet as she sat trying to become engaged in the church service, she now doubted that her timing had been appropriate. She could see Nick sitting on the other side of the church with his boys. She wondered if he had seen the note. If he had, what was he thinking? Would he avoid her or approach her after the service? She hoped he hadn't seen it yet, but would find it when he arrived home. Maybe she should have told Nolan not to let his father see the paper until after church. Still, hadn't she already given the five-year-old enough to handle?

Nick wondered whether or not he should approach Charlotte after church or wait until he had more time to think about things. He knew what he intended to say, but the church hardly seemed the location for their discussion. Besides, Charlotte may not have been expecting him to see the note until after he had gone home. Although his heart was in disagreement, Nick decided the conversation would have to wait.

"Is something wrong, dear?" Charlotte's mother could detect trouble from several hundred miles away. She noticed how disappointed her daughter's greeting had been on the phone and how short her answers were. Apparently she had been hoping for another call. Although Charlotte wished to conceal the truth from her mother, she also longed for the counsel of the woman she had always desired to imitate. She didn't think her mother would have stooped so low as to have a preschooler deliver a message that should have been brought in person, but then her mother never would have quarreled in the first place when she knew what her true feelings were. Charlotte's desire for consolation and understanding momentarily outweighed her pride, and in the space of a few minutes, she had filled her mother in on all the significant details of the past several months. Mrs. Sanders was silent until Charlotte had finished.

"So all this has been going on? I don't really know what to say." Charlotte could have wished for a more favorable reaction from her mother. Was it so difficult to believe that she'd been offered the opportunity to pursue another relationship?

"Well, what do you think about how I've reacted to the whole ordeal?" Charlotte asked, frustration wearing her voice thin. "I've made a mess of everything, haven't I?"

"I don't know if I would say that," Mrs. Sanders replied steadily. "You don't know how things will turn out yet. It's the waiting that's the most difficult."

Charlotte's mother took an opportunity to catch her breath. "You went through a lot when you lost Peter, Charlotte. You seemed to take it well, but I always wondered if something in you never was quite able to get over it. I had always hoped you would marry. When you moved away, I thought that it might help you move on with life. I'm not saying that you were wrong, I'm just saying that maybe you haven't faced everything as you thought you had. Maybe you haven't had a reason to until now." Charlotte hadn't thought much about what her mother's expectations for her life had been. She had never voiced her desire for Charlotte to marry. Charlotte had resigned herself to the role of an aunt years before, but apparently her mother had hoped to see her as something more. For a moment, Charlotte speculated how things might have been different had she followed the expectations of others. Then she brought herself back to the present; such *might-have-beens* were not worth considering now.

"Why don't I let you go for now?" Charlotte's mother asked, with every intention of freeing the phone line as soon as possible. "Your answer might be trying to reach you right now, but I'm in the way."

"You're never in the way, Mom," Charlotte responded fondly. "I know it didn't sound like it at first, but I'm glad you called. I'll let you know how everything works out."

"You'd better!" was the severe reply. "I don't want to receive a wedding invitation in the mail without warning."

"I don't think things will move that fast!" Charlotte laughed for the first time that evening. Although nothing had changed, Charlotte's heart felt lighter than it did at the beginning of their conversation. *Moms have a way of doing that for their daughters,* Charlotte thought to herself.

After saying goodbye, Charlotte went away to prepare her lesson for her school children. She had barely worked through a page of material before the phone again interrupted her work. She answered it hesitantly; it was in times like these that she wondered at her failure to invest in Caller ID. Although Charlotte had been looking forward to a call from Nick all evening, she now dreaded a conversation with him. Still, she was engaged in one before she had much of an opportunity to do anything else.

"Nolan brought home some interesting papers today," Nick commented, after he and Charlotte exchanged greetings. He hardly knew how to broach the subject, but figured it would be best to ease into it.

"Yes," Charlotte responded dumbly, unable to think of anything else to say. She was grateful when Nick resumed the conversation and gave her a minute to allow her rapidly beating heart to steady into a more even rhythm.

"I admire your resourcefulness," Nick admitted. "I know I tried to make myself unapproachable, but you found a way to get through to me."

"And you're okay with that?" Charlotte asked, still a little unsure of Nick's current feelings toward her. She didn't suppose that he had called to lecture her about how she had handled the situation, but she couldn't feel quite at ease until she knew for sure what he was thinking.

"I'm more than okay with that," Nick responded warmly. "I wish I hadn't made it so hard on you, but then again it makes me feel pretty good to be so sought after." Charlotte knew she could relax now. After all her doubts, her plan was shaping up to be a successful one. Charlotte remembered the tone of voice Nick had used before when he had called to share his true feelings. She had thought of it often in the past few days, and was delighted to hear Nick speak to her again with the same sincerity.

"I gather from your note that you've changed your mind about me?" Nick made his statement sound a little like a question, even though he felt sure of the answer he'd receive.

"Yes," Charlotte responded, again at a loss for anything more intelligent to say.

"So would you like to go out to dinner this weekend?"

"I'd love to." Charlotte could not believe what was happening to her. Yes, she had once had a serious relationship, but that was a long time ago. Here she was in the middle of her life, feeling excited, unsure, and restless like a teenage girl. She was so wrapped up in her newfound feelings and anticipations that she couldn't follow Nick's new line of thought.

"You know what this means, don't you?" he asked, his voice low and seemingly serious. If only Charlotte could have seen the twinkle in his eyes, she would have realized that he meant no harm. As it was, she found his question a little unsettling.

"No, what does it mean?"

"I'm going to have to find another babysitter!"

Twenty-Five

Jared

Helen breathed a sigh of contentment as she surveyed the room before her. The sun had set more than an hour previous, and the space was now illuminated by candles and lights set dim to mimic the effect. The frosted strands encircling the Christmas tree seemed to match the windowpanes, which glistened with their own, frosty decoration. Krissie, Alex, and their cousins were gathered around the tree, playing with different toys they had received earlier in the day. Maddy and Kevin were seated at a card table, playing a board game with their aunt and uncle. Timothy was savoring the opportunity to hold his sleeping grandson. Although there was a significant deal of conversation taking place, it did not detract from the serenity of the room as each person spoke using low and careful tones.

Helen had just taken a seat beside her husband when a thought struck her. Looking once again about the room as if in hopes of discovering something new, she asked Timothy, "Where's Molly?" Timothy shrugged his shoulders. Although he didn't know exactly where his daughter had retreated, he felt that retreat had been her object. He'd seen her sad eyes search the room earlier and find only vacancy. After allowing Timothy to watch Ethan, Molly had disappeared down the hall.

Recognizing the message her husband's eyes seemed to convey, Helen anxiously rose from her seat. Although she recognized that Molly likely needed her space, she couldn't bear to think of her daughter bearing her burden all alone.

Peeking into the room at the end of the hall, Helen's suspicions were confirmed. Molly had sought her old bedroom as a refuge. At first the room seemed silent; yet the longer she stood, the more Helen could distinguish the faint whimpers of one who had exceeded her capacity for bravery.

In an instant Helen was at Molly's side, stroking her hair now slightly matted by tears. While Molly had hoped to keep her burden to herself, she knew she had failed to shut the door, perhaps in hope that her mother might come to check on her. Although she knew no explanation was necessary for her mother to understand, she offered one nonetheless.

"I'm sorry, Mom, but I can't..." Molly choked as the words she had repressed throughout the day seemed to now come only with the pain that accompanied having held them inside. "I can't force myself to be happy when he's not here. This is the second Christmas we've been apart. It makes me wonder when we'll ever be together." Molly stopped herself from proceeding any further. She heard remnants of despondency in the tone of her own voice, and it almost scared her. So many times in the past she'd been able to cope with her situation without giving in to bitterness or despair. Living on her own, it was perhaps necessary for her own health and well-being, not to mention Ethan's, to refrain from giving full exercise to her emotions. It had been easier to carry on before the holidays, when there was less pressure to assume a false position of happiness. Around Christmastime, however, it seemed like everyone had a role to play, whether she cared to or not.

Helen trusted that her daughter would rally in time, but she felt the need to offer some gentle words of advice. She failed to address the words she knew Molly didn't mean. The entire family was aware that Jared would be returning any day now. What could not be altered was what had passed. Jared and Molly had spent the majority of their marriage apart. The two would almost be starting all over again when Jared came home, only this time Ethan would be part of their lives.

"We didn't invite you for Christmas so that you could pretend to be happy and content, Molly," Helen explained quietly. "Even if you were to pretend, your father and I would know better. We know you're hurting, not only for Jared, but for all that seems to have been lost this last year and a half." Helen's words seemed to resonate within Molly's soul, giving semblance to emotions that had appeared coded in an unknown script. Although Molly had known the difficulties that might await her when she married Jared, and had considered them of less weight than the reality of a long engagement, she had seen in the time since her marriage why others had been concerned about her choice. Still, she couldn't regret marrying Jared when she did. She loved him so much and had been determined that the things that affected him would affect her. If it seemed difficult to think of herself waiting alone till Jared's return before their marriage, it was worse to imagine Jared overseas without the motivation of coming home to a family on his return. *Family.* That's what they were, and since Jared had left, their family had grown. If Molly hadn't married Jared when she did, they wouldn't have had Ethan. The little boy had been such a blessing to Molly while his father was away. Ethan had brought Molly joy and hope at times when she needed them most.

"I guess Jared and I have lost some things since we married like we did," Molly restated, before quickly adding, "but we've gained a lot too. We have a son to raise, and the time we have together will be more special since it's been so rare. It's hard not to think of what might have been, but Jared will be home soon. That's all that matters."

Helen nodded her head slowly. There was more that she wished to share, but her lips were sealed.

Just as the Evergreen's Christmas gathering was drawing to a close, a knock was heard at the door. Several of the children, who had just moments before been struggling to stay awake, looked excitedly at each other with puzzled glances. Their faces said that they had already thought their assembly complete. Once Timothy had shown their new guest into the living room, however, the children quickly found they had room for at least one more.

"Ho, ho, ho!" a familiar character heralded as he entered the room. "Merry Christmas!" The traditional red suit seemed to draw the children to itself like a magnet. It was all Santa could do to acknowledge his little admirers, let alone answer their numerous questions.

Although the visitor was dressed like Santa Claus, arrayed in the characteristically red stuffed suit, matching hat, and black boots, and wearing a long, white beard, little else about him was very convincing. His voice seemed to alternate between medium and low tones, the latter being quickly assumed after lapses into the former. Despite the white hair and beard that framed the man's face, every other indication of age typified a much younger individual. No wrinkles were to be found underneath the turquoise-blue eyes, which seemed to twinkle the same way Santa Claus' might. Although the lighting was poor in the room where the family was gathered, any acute observer might have thought the man's complexion was rather dark considering he supposedly spent his time out-of-doors at the North Pole. Still, the children welcomed him with open arms. Whether or not they considered him to be the actual Claus, their parents couldn't strictly determine.

The man had brought a bag of toys with him, but he had purposely left it in the other room. Krissie and Alex were more than eager to help out. They excitedly ran into the other room, arguing as to who would be more responsible for bearing the load of the sack's weight. They had quieted by the time they re-entered the room, however, realizing that their parents were alert, even on Christmas Day.

It seemed that Santa Claus had a present for every individual or couple. After passing out a round of gifts, he paused.

“Where’s Ethan Weaver?” he asked suddenly.

Molly started at the mention of her son’s name. Although she had been watching events transpire, her mind had been miles away. She had taken no more notice of their visitor than she might have of a fictional character on television or in a book. As to his identity, she easily assumed him to be one of the men from her parents’ church. Since she had been away from their church for a while, she didn’t necessarily expect to recognize him. She was surprised that he had prepared a gift for her son. She had not been given a present with the others, and she didn’t want or expect one, yet it was sweet to think of Ethan getting a present from Santa Claus on his first Christmas. Molly’s heart rapidly became a little lighter, as she brushed aside her reflections to show the man where her son lay sleeping in a crib beside the Christmas tree. She was surprised when Santa delayed presenting his gift, but instead stood gazing intently at the little child. His eyes appeared softened and almost moist with repressed tears. In a moment, however, he recovered himself, and handed Molly a package. She opened it to find a stuffed baby blue elephant with Ethan’s name stitched into it.

“Thank you, Santa,” Molly said, while only momentarily lifting her eyes to focus on the recipient of her words. As she did, a new thought entered into her mind, but she instantly brushed it aside. *Impossible!* Her mind was playing tricks on her.

“Pick me up, Santa! Pick me up!” Krissie's cousin, Stephen, cried. A thought had just occurred to him and he instantly acted on it. Stephen secretly wondered if Santa might be hiding some extra goodies in his coat pocket. If so, the best spot to be would be in Santa’s arms.

Although he expected to be swept up immediately, Stephen was disappointed. Instead of reaching for the boy, Santa just stood there looking at him. His beard moved as his lips fumbled to give some sort of explanation. Meanwhile, Molly stood by with a growing conviction in her heart that her ridiculous idea might not be so wrong after all. One long look into the eyes of the man revealed his identity. Without thinking, Molly pulled down the false beard that hid her from her husband and kissed him. Immediately, Stephen burst into tears. It was not Santa after all! Glad to be freed from the constraints of his role and part of his costume, Jared pulled off his hat before pulling Molly closer to himself. Even while he returned her long kiss, he fought to believe the reality of which he was a part. He was home! After all this time, he was actually home!

"I didn't bring you a present other than myself," Jared said, after he felt able to descend the heights of his inexpressible happiness in order to talk. "I hope you don't mind."

"Mind?" Molly asked with tears in her eyes. "This is the best Christmas present I've ever had!"

Although Molly and Jared had momentarily forgotten the other people in the room, they now included their family in their joy. Krissie and Alex surrounded Jared and instantly began asking him questions.

As she looked about the room, Molly spotted her mother standing a distance away. Molly smiled as she considered how Helen always seemed to know what she needed. Earlier when Molly had despaired of seeing Jared, Helen had been there to mourn with her. Now that Jared had come, she rejoiced, but at a respectful distance.

Crossing the room, Molly wrapped her arms around Helen. Both were in tears, but their tears were some of the happiest they had ever known. As Molly looked back at Jared, she saw him kneeling down by his son, the son he had only seen in pictures. Ethan began to stir a little and Jared caught the small hand he had started to flail. At their first engaging sight of each other, both Jared and Ethan seemed mesmerized. Jared even thought he saw a smile on his son's face.

Try as he might, Jared could not maintain his composure. Retrieving the hand he had offered to Ethan, he buried his face in his hands and wept. In no time, Molly was at his side and the three had the room completely to themselves.

“I’ve dreamed of this day for months,” Jared admitted to Molly after the room had cleared. “I can’t believe I’m finally home, with you and Ethan. My heart has been here all along.”

“I’m so glad you’re home,” Molly whispered. This time Jared looked up to gaze into her eyes and echo her sentiments in a lingering kiss.

Twenty-Six

The Christmas Holidays

For the first time since moving away from her hometown, Charlotte prepared to spend a Christmas with her family. In the past, she had always avoided visiting during the holidays, since they seemed to bring back difficult memories. Charlotte had never trusted herself before to be in very high spirits during, what was supposed to be, this merry time of year. Yet, since Nick Parker's entrance in her life, things were different. How different they might become, she could only wonder.

Charlotte's mother and brothers were extremely interested in meeting Nick and his boys, and had invited them to visit during Christmas along with Charlotte. While Nick was already engaged to spend Christmas with Karen's parents in Indiana, he arranged to make a short trip through Illinois on his way back to Missouri after the holiday.

Although Charlotte had felt her confidence rising since beginning a serious relationship with Nick, she still wrestled with various insecurities. During the time Nick spent with her family, she couldn't help feeling awkward and on display. It was one thing for a young woman to have her boyfriend visit her family; it was an entirely different matter to have a widower with two small children come home to meet the folks. Still, from all outward appearances, no one else seemed to mind. Charlotte's family quickly fell in love with Tristan and Nolan and tried to make Nick feel right at home.

The only wonder to Nick was how Charlotte could have left such a wonderful family. He pondered the question over and over, until an all too familiar explanation presented itself. He, of all people, had no right to blame Charlotte for how she had reacted to her situation. He had left behind wonderful in-laws who regretted being so far away from their son-in-law and two grandsons. How ironic it was that they had reacted the same way to their circumstances and managed to find each other at the end of them!

On the last day of his visit with the Sanders family, Nick found Charlotte sitting quietly in the library, which had become a makeshift guest room for her. Curled up in a comfortable chair situated in the bay window, Charlotte was staring out across the empty, snow-filled cornfields. Although wintry air leaked in around the window, Charlotte kept warm by taking frequent sips of her hot chocolate. Every now and then, she was forced to avert her eyes from the window as a ream of bright sunlight came bursting through the low mountain of clouds. During one such instance, Charlotte turned and was startled to see Nick standing in the doorway of the room. She was not sure how long he had been watching her. He seemed deep in thought, and his puzzled expression caused him to look as though he were lost. Charlotte smiled warmly at him, feeling the pace of her heart quicken as he returned her smile.

"Are you looking for something?" Charlotte didn't know why after the last few comfortable days she had spent with Nick, she now felt anxious. It was just the way he kept staring at her.

"Yeah," Nick muttered under his breath. "Do you mind if I join you?" he said more audibly.

"Not at all. Pull up a chair." Charlotte gestured to a folding chair that was placed in an out of the way corner. Nick hesitated for a moment to speak or move, but then slowly began to explain himself as he drew nearer to Charlotte.

"I don't think I'll be needing that," he began, before kneeling down in front of her. Charlotte gasped, almost choking on the amount of air she quickly inhaled. She knew she would only need to speak one word when the time came; still, she struggled to prepare herself.

"I don't know what you've been expecting, or what you've hoped for in a proposal," Nick admitted, stumbling over his words. "Maybe I should have asked," he continued, crinkling his dark eyebrows in uncertainty. "But I wanted to surprise you. I hope you know how much I care for you...and love you." Saying this much, Nick reached for Charlotte's left hand. She gave it up willingly, as the tears began to spill over her cheeks. "Charlotte, will you marry me?"

Charlotte could not keep herself from crying, but allowing her sparkling eyes to meet Nick's, she responded in both word and look. Nick slipped a ring onto her finger before standing to catch her up in his arms. Both were so entranced in the moment that they initially failed to hear the loud rhythm of stomping behind them. Soon, however, Nick turned around to look out the open doorway into the hall. There he saw Tristan and Nolan, removing their snow encrusted boots at the instruction of one of Charlotte's brothers. Once they were free to do so, the boys came running into the room where Nick and Charlotte stood and Tristan began tattling on his younger brother.

"Dad, Nolan went sliding down a hill he wasn't supposed to when Mr. Sanders wasn't looking," he said, pleased to be a bearer of bad tidings.

"I didn't know I wasn't supposed to," Nolan asserted in his own defense.

"You would've if you'd paid attention," Tristan lectured, before abruptly ending his arguments as he caught the solemn look of his father.

"We'll deal with this later," Nick decided, amazed at how quickly he could assume his fatherly role after asking Charlotte to marry him. "Right now we have other things to do." Nick looked at Charlotte and gave her hand a gentle squeeze. She gazed lovingly back at him and then at the mischievous boys that she would someday soon call her own. Tristan and Nolan glanced back and forth between the couple and each other, both searching for hints as to their father's meaning.

"What do you mean?" Tristan volunteered.

"We have some news to spread," Nick informed his son. His face was beaming with happiness as he thought of the future that awaited him and his boys.

"What news?" Nolan chimed in, crinkling up his small nose that was still red from being outside in the cold.

"Well," Nick began, "Miss Charlotte and I are going to be married!" He spoke enthusiastically, but his boys needed no extra encouragement. After looking at each other, they cried out in delight and ran to embrace their two favorite people.

Nick and Charlotte were delighted with their reactions, but they were forced to choke when Nolan asked, "Are you going to get married today?"

"No, son," Nick responded simply, "not today."

Twenty-Seven

Heather

Although there were a few incidents that Jared chose not to share with anyone, save Molly, he was otherwise extremely open concerning his time in Iraq. He was almost eager to tell others about the event which caused his injury, since in spite of the close proximity of the explosive, there was no loss of life. Jared saw it as a magnificent example of divine protection and it gave him ample opportunities to share his faith.

When Molly suggested to Jared that they invite their neighbors over to dinner some evening, Jared quickly agreed. He was extremely grateful to Heather for all the help she had been to Molly during his time away and he was anxious for company in general.

Terry and Heather came over the following weekend. It was apparent that they were both surprised by Jared's behavior. Terry especially had been prepared to find Jared out-of-humor and even angry about what had happened. Instead Jared seemed even more cheerful and optimistic than he remembered. He was puzzled and wondered if it had anything to do with the faith he kept mentioning.

After dinner the couples assembled in the Weaver's small living room for games. It wasn't long before the oven let out a series of beeps.

"I better go get the brownies," Molly said, standing up and excusing herself.

“It’s about time,” Jared teased, “that smell was starting to get to me.” Molly rolled her eyes and started for the kitchen.

“Do you mind if I come with you?” Heather asked, her voice a little shaky. Molly read uneasiness in her friend’s eyes and she was concerned. She told Heather she would welcome her help and the two walked away together. Molly could only guess what was on Heather’s mind and she wondered that Terry hadn't seemed to notice.

“Did you want to talk?” Molly asked Heather after removing the brownie tray from the oven. She spoke in a whisper, knowing her words could be overheard if she spoke in her usual voice. Heather nodded silently in response. Since it was the middle of winter, Molly knew that the back porch was out of the question for an alternative place of conversation. Suggesting they head back to her bedroom, Molly led Heather to the back of the house, hoping that her friend would be more open once she knew that her voice would be out of hearing. Her plan worked and Heather began speaking almost as soon as Molly had shut the door behind them.

“I’m glad you could tell I needed to talk,” Heather admitted, her eyes cast down. “Something’s been weighing on my mind all evening.”

“What?” Molly asked, stepping forward to lay her hand on Heather’s shoulder. When Heather looked up, tears were shining in her eyes. She didn’t know where to begin, but she knew she couldn’t conceal her burden any longer.

“I want what you and Jared have,” Heather revealed at last. Although she thought that her point might be taken from her words, she was mistaken. Molly could only think of one apparent meaning and, at first, she became a little angry at her friend. Molly and Jared had only been experiencing parenthood together for a few weeks now. Why Heather would choose to be envious of them, Molly could not determine. She only felt she was the wrong person to be involved in this conversation.

“Have you talked to Terry about this?” she asked gently.

"No, he's even less open to religion than I have been." Heather spoke honestly, yet there was a residual sadness in her tone. As she paused to look up at Molly, Heather read the surprise in her face.

"What exactly are you talking about?" Molly inquired, although she was beginning to see what Heather meant.

"Well, I know you've invited me to go to church with you before," Heather began, "but I've never wanted to go. I've always had an excuse, but mainly I just didn't think I needed to go. I don't know, but somehow listening to Jared talk tonight about God...it's so different than anything I've heard before. I've believed there is a God, but you guys talk about Him like He's your next door neighbor or something."

"No, you're my next door neighbor," Molly chimed in, a reassuring smile on her face. Although she had prayed for her friend for months, she had never seen any change in her before. Her heart was racing with excitement and anticipation. She silently prayed for the Lord to guide her words. "Jesus is my Savior. He's concerned about every detail of my life and Jared's. There isn't anything that comes into our lives that He hasn't foreseen and allowed. We don't always know why they happen, but we can trust that He has a reason."

"I guess some people can see it that way," Heather commented casually, shrugging her shoulders. "I've never been one of them. Different truths comfort different people." Heather felt the lameness of her words even as she said them.

"But can they all be true?" Molly asked simply.

Heather was a little taken aback. "What do you mean?" It was apparent that she had not thought all of her own beliefs through as Molly perhaps had.

"Different religions have different ways of getting to heaven, but God has only ordained one way. He sent His Son to earth to pay the penalty for our sins so that we could spend eternity with Him. Jesus said He was 'the way, the truth, and the life'. If we believe that, there can be no other truth." Molly tried to speak as powerfully as she could, but she knew that she could never persuade someone to believe God's Word. Only the Holy Spirit could do that. Yet, Heather considered her words thoughtfully. Having a husband who, as she said, did not care to discuss spiritual matters, Heather had not considered many of these things before. She momentarily wondered how she could have had so many experiences in life and failed to carefully address the greatest question of all.

"I guess I've never really thought about it much before," she admitted at last.

"Can I ask you another question?" Heather could tell from the look in Molly's eyes that she wasn't merely trying to persuade her to see things her way; Molly was concerned about her friend's welfare. It occurred to Heather that Molly was speaking in the same gentle manner Jared had used when relating his experiences in Iraq. What was it that made them so different, that brought them such peace in the midst of trying transitions? Whatever it was, Heather was forced to acknowledge that it wasn't a part of her own life. After receiving permission from Heather to continue, Molly asked her question.

"Do you have peace?" The four words drove deep into Heather's soul, bringing up images of events she had tried to forget. All at once she remembered the depression she had experienced as a teenager in high school after her father passed away. Although it had been the most devastating era of her life, Heather knew there were other periods when she had wrestled with situations, resigning herself to each only as a necessity of moving on. Yet, there were no answers to any of her questions. There was no assurance that things had happened for specific reasons that were all part of a loving God's plan. While Heather did not expect that Molly could provide answers to some of the questions that still plagued her heart from time to time, she could not resist the desire to learn more of Molly's secret strength.

"No, not like you have," she answered at last, her eyes filled with tears at her recollections.

"Would you like to?" Again, four simple words seemed to cut to Heather's heart. How could it be so simple? How could Molly simply offer peace like it were a keepsake in her home that she felt free to give away?

"Yes." Heather wasn't sure that she had spoken her answer out loud, yet found she must have when Molly began to share with her what she had wished to share all along.

"Good," Molly breathed excitingly, with a reassuring nod of her head. "Jesus has offered His peace to all people. If you will ask Him to forgive you from your sins and seek to walk with Him for the rest of your life, you will find great peace. Jesus provided the payment for your sins by His death on the cross. All you have to do is accept what He's freely given to you."

"How can I get Him to listen to me?" Heather asked, still not sure things could be so simple.

"He's listening now," Molly replied. She watched as Heather closed her eyes and prayed. She could not discern her words, but she could see her lips moving. When she next looked up, Molly could see that Heather's expression had changed. Her look was one of relief and great joy. Molly instantly moved toward her friend and hugged her.

"Did you ask Him?" she inquired.

"Yeah, I did." Heather responded simply.

Twenty-Eight

"I Do"

For a moment, a ray of April sunshine bursting through the church's stained glass window fell upon a figure arrayed in white as she stepped lightly down the aisle. She walked alone; her father had passed on some years before. Although she wished he could have been present to give her away, she felt sure she would have had his blessing.

Focusing her gaze upon her mother, Charlotte was startled to see her already holding a handkerchief to her eyes. In an effort to maintain her composure, she quickly looked across to her beloved. His eyes too seemed moist, but his rich smile sent joy coursing through Charlotte. Although she had missed most of Nolan's trek down the aisle, Charlotte now glanced at her soon-to-be son as he proudly held the ring pillow. Charlotte wondered what she had done to deserve such happiness, before quickly realizing it had nothing to do with her at all. The Giver of all good gifts had been gracious to them. What a wonderful God they served! Just then Nick took Charlotte's hands in his and the minister began his address.

The Evergreen family followed the ceremony from their seats a few rows behind the happy couple. Timothy and Helen remained awestruck by the turn of events that had led to this day. They remembered first meeting Nick and his boys and how withdrawn and sorrowful they had been at the time. Now their only tears were tears of joy. Helen couldn't help but feel a little satisfaction that she had urged Charlotte toward her groom. Still, she knew that such a beautiful story as theirs belonged to a much more talented Author than herself.

Maddy Evergreen watched intently, dwelling on each challenge given and promise made. She couldn't help wondering when her day would come and found herself distracted by the friend who sat beside her. Had she been too quick in diverting his attentions toward her? Since their conversation at Krissie's birthday party, Wesley had been nothing more than friendly. Was that how she truly wanted things to stand between them? Maddy sighed lightly before focusing again on the ceremony. She would just have to wait to see what the Lord had in store for them.

Krissie's mind was also full of romance, but with an added touch of anxiety. Tristan Parker would be staying at her house for the next week and a half while his parents were away. Unknown to the rest of her family, Krissie had developed a crush on the boy, and how would it be to have him staying at her home? Would Tristan pal around with Alex, who teased her without end? What if Tristan teased her too? Krissie swallowed hard; she just knew she would never be able to live it down.

With beaming smiles the couple turned to face the gathered crowd as the pastor pronounced them “Mr. and Mrs. Nicolas Parker”. The guests soon followed them into the church's large fellowship hall for refreshments. It was there that Nolan approached his father with a wide grin stretched across face.

“Daddy,” he said, while pulling on one of the tails of his father's suit.

“Yes, Nolan, what is it?” Nick asked, excusing himself to the friend who had also been talking to him.

“I don't think our house will look so ugly anymore,” the boy responded with glee.

“No...I think it will be beautiful from now on.” Nick looked across the hall to his new wife. He caught her eye and beaming smile. Reaching down to catch his son in his arms,

Nick tossed Nolan's hair until he protested. Just then the guests began pounding on their tables in unison. Letting Nolan to the ground, Nick crossed the room to his bride and swept her back for a long kiss. Charlotte was speechless.